BANDEMIC

FRESHH MONEYY

URBAN AINT DEAD PRESENTS

URBAN AINT DEAD

P.O Box 448

Maybrook, NY 12543

Cover Design: P. Wise / The Wise Services

Edited By: Shawna Brim / Ladies of Lit

Contact Publisher at www.urbanaintdead.com

Email: urbanaintdead@gmail.com

Print ISBN: 979-8-9908882-6-5

STAY UP TO DATE

To stay up to date on new releases, plus get information on contests, sneak peeks and more,

Click the link below...
https://mailchi.mp/6d21003686d1/subscribe

SOUNDTRACKS

Scan the QR Code below to listen to the Soundtracks/Singles of some of your favorite U.A.D titles:

Don't have Spotify or Apple Music?
No Sweat!
Visit your choice streaming platform and search URBAN AINT DEAD.

Currently on lock serving a bid?
JPay, iHeartRadio, WHATEVER!
We got you covered.
Simply log into your facility's kiosk or tablet, go to music and search
URBAN AINT DEAD.

URBAN AINT DEAD PRESENTS

Like & Follow us on social media:

FB - URBAN AINT DEAD

IG: @uadpresents

Tik Tok - @uadpresents

Submission Guidelines

Submit the first three chapters of your completed manuscript to
urbanaintdead@gmail.com, subject line: Your book's title. The
manuscript must be in a .doc file and sent as an attachment. The
document should be in Times New Roman, double-spaced, and in size
12 font. Also, provide your synopsis and full contact information. If
sending multiple submissions, they must each be in a separate email.
Have a story but no way to submit it electronically? You can still
submit to URBAN AINT DEAD. Send in the first three chapters,
written or typed, of your completed manuscript to:

URBAN AINT DEAD
P.O Box 448
Maybrook, NY 12543

DO NOT send original manuscript. Must be a duplicate.
Provide your synopsis and a cover letter containing your full contact
information.
Thanks for considering URBAN AINT DEAD.

ACKNOWLEDGMENTS

I was once told, "You're not a mediocre nigga," and it was hands down the best compliment and most motivational statement I've ever received. I hold it dear, and it helped me want better for myself. Cocoloso, you took your sweet ass time, but you were the first to type this book up and got it where It needed to go. I appreciate you, my boy. The UAD family, thank you for the opportunity and assistance in sharing my art with the world. I won't disappoint you. For those who supported me and for those who doubted me, look at me now. Ya are equally appreciated.

January 16, 2009

The vibration of the Blackberry Curve against the wooden nightstand indicated an incoming call and pulled the attention of the duo from the TV screen. The Sidekick LX lying next to it hadn't alerted with any AIM messages, and it was about two in the morning, so this call had to be important.

Dream sucked her teeth in annoyance. "This is my favorite part," she whined as the *Baby Boy* DVD played.

Prince watched as Jodi accepted Rodney's collect call and scoffed. "I would of broke your jaw," he commented, causing her to giggle before he sat between her legs, leaned over, and grabbed his phone. The call was from his right-hand man, Kasper. "Sup, bro?" Prince answered as he moved to his side of the bed.

"Heard a lot of noise close by... just checking up on you, my brother," Kasper responded before taking a pull of the Newport.

Gunshots. The East New York section of Brooklyn spoke gun talk fluently, and as of late, it had become Prince's favorite language. Prince Smith was just four months shy of his fifteenth birthday. But the young boy was doing grown man things. He had been born and raised in the hood, so he wasn't slipping or slacking in the streets. He had caught his first body a year prior, and another followed soon after. Ever since then, he and his pistol were best friends. So, Kasper wasn't concerned with his safety; it was Prince's freedom he worried about. The pretty boy had become a killer, and it was scary to witness. He had always been the topic of conversation due to his looks and drip, but nowadays, his name was associated with nothing but gunplay.

Two years ago, Prince and his older brother were known as the Pretty Boy Family. They were the flyest, were well known, and because of their Yemeni, Jamaican, and Puerto Rican nationality, they stood out. They were chill back then, but then, Prince's older brother, Pretty Boy, was murdered by a hating nigga over a bitch. Then, the war started, and it was a war Prince didn't plan on losing. Him and his niggas had become flagitious and now had a team of demons that called themselves Forever Famous.

"I'm laid up, bout to step out in a few though," he informed Kasper. Prince felt movement behind him on the bed before Dream's hands moved around his shoulders and down his chest as her lips landed on his neck tattoo. "Where you at?"

"Front of the chicken spot. It's bricks ass out here," Kasper said as he inspected his surroundings. The winter wind was biting, but the money didn't sleep or stop, so every night, Kasper bundled up and posted, acting as a twenty-four-hour pharmacist for the crackheads and dope fiends. At sixteen years old, Kasper wasn't hustling for recreation; he did it to survive.

"I got a Montclair and a heater. I'ma be aight," Prince cracked but was serious. "Meet me at the diner so we could grab some food after I bust this move." Kasper flicked his cigarette then tucked his hand in his North Face jacket.

"Cool, bro," he said before ending the call.

Prince turned his attention to Dream. "Start getting ready. It's already two."

Dream traced his neck tattoo with her pierced tongue. "Okay, baby." She pecked at his neck before climbing out of the bed. Prince's eyes instantly went to her panty covered backside as she pulled the wedgie out with her manicured fingers, causing her butt cheeks to jiggle.

Dream was a catch, and everything that she did was enticing. At eighteen years old, she was a wifey type, a butter pecan Puerto Rican with a body like a Benz. Her eyes were the lightest shade of brown, her dimples were prominent, and her lips were pink and pouty. Her black hair with the brown streaks cascaded down to her lower back, and although she hated it, Prince had a fetish for pulling hair, so she would never cut it. Dream's friends told her she was crazy for messing with someone so young, but her love for Prince outweighed her judgment.

When they first met, Dream was a cashier at a supermarket. Tired of the minimum wage way of living, she had somehow someway taught herself the art of scamming. Now, Dream splurged using bogus credit cards, gift cards, and using fraudulent business checks. Once her hustle took off, the first thing she did was put Prince on. He was considered next up, so it was only right that he cuffed the one everybody wanted. Dream and Prince had been together for seven months, and his nights in her bed were more frequent than the ones in his own. They were inseparable, and that wasn't changing anytime soon.

Prince stood and began to dress too, throwing on a pair of Taverniti jeans, a rugby polo shirt and hoodie, then a BB Simon belt and Polo field boots, while Dream decided on a grey sweatsuit by PINK and a pair of Asolos. Prince grabbed his .45 from her sock drawer, and as much as Dream wanted to say something, she bit her tongue, knowing he wouldn't leave without it. *At least he didn't take both of them*, she justified. Prince tucked the gun in his waist and pecked Dream's cheek as she brushed her hair. "Hurry up." He rushed her as she walked out of her bedroom and into the dimly lit, smoke-filled living room. "Fuck ya still doing up?" Prince asked as she fanned in front of his face.

When Dream leased her apartment, she had allowed her younger sister, Abby, to tag along. At fifteen years old, Abby was a hot in the ass beauty. Prince and Abby attended the same school, and she was the one who had put Dream on to who he was. Since everybody knew Dream was with Prince, they chased Abby, and she gladly ate up the attention. So, it wasn't surprising to see Banko, a seventeen-year-old hustler from the hood, lounging on the couch, sharing a blunt with Abby. The question was directed at Prince's left-hand man, Money, and Prince's little cousin, Mike-Mike. One had run away from home, and the other had been kicked out, so Prince had allowed them to crash in Dream's living room.

"What's popping, bro?" Banko spoke to Prince. Prince acknowledged him with a head nod as he grabbed his jacket off the couch. Although Banko ran with the older niggas from Prince's side, Prince didn't fuck with him. Banko was originally from the op side where the niggas that killed Pretty Boy were from, and the only reason Prince hadn't done anything to Banko was off the strength of Prince's father, War. Banko had hustled for him, and War let niggas know that Banko was good on his side. War had run the hood for years, and even Prince's mother had done her one twos.

Unfortunately, War had recently gotten locked up, charged with a double homicide, and was sitting on Rikers Island fighting the case.

"I'm going with you, bro." Money jumped up, breaking the tension. He knew how his mans felt about Banko and how quickly he would act off emotions. Banko smirked knowingly and sat unfazed as he watched Dream walk into the living room then leave with Prince, Money, and Mike-Mike.

"What's wrong?" Abby asked, eyebrows dipping in concern.

"Nothing, boo," he said as he dug in his pocket and removed a bag containing E pills. "Roll with me."

A LITTLE OVER AN HOUR LATER, THEY SAT IN THE RIDGEWOOD KATS Diner, enjoying an early breakfast. The bank transactions had gone smoothly as usual. Prince and Dream's pockets were a few bands heavier. Prince looked from Kasper to Money to Mike-Mike and grinned. If there was one thing that he loved, it was his team. They were quickly becoming the talk of the town, and their bond was solid. They were the only motherfuckers that he trusted.

"I got it," Dream said, breaking him out of his train of thought as she grabbed the checkbook from the waitress. She pulled out a crispy $50 bill and placed it inside the checkbook. Dream had cleared $1,700 twice, totaling $3,400, ate a good meal, and now just wanted to get home and cuddle with her man. The smile on her face couldn't be contained.

"Good looking, sis." Kasper thanked her as he stuffed the last of his home fries in his mouth. "Yo, my brother, I need you to come with me to re-up too."

The smile on Dream's face instantly dipped because she knew nothing – or no one – could stop Prince from riding with or for his niggas.

"When, bro?" Prince responded just as she expected.

"I'm dry. I already hit dogs, so he up waiting." Kasper shrugged.

"Why can't Money or Mike-Mike go?" Dream hissed, her attitude apparent.

Ignoring her attitude, Prince stood from his seat. "Cause we could all go. I'll meet you at the crib."

Thirty minutes later, the four were getting off the J train on Van Siclen Street, and a chill ran through Prince's body. They were only seven blocks from his own, but this was the same block his brother had been murdered on. They walked through the snow and into an apartment building where Kasper walked inside an apartment to conduct his business while they waited in the hallway. Prince had never sold a drug before, so he couldn't understand why Kasper wouldn't transition from drug dealer to scamming like he constantly advised. He would never understand that selling drugs was like smoking them – highly addictive.

"You alright, cuzzo?" Mike-Mike asked Prince, whose blood boiled more by the second. Money watched him closely as well. None of them could relate to the emotions stampeding through him. The apartment door opened, and Kasper walked out.

"Come on, bro. We gone." He threw his arm around Prince's shoulders as they exited the building. Prince scanned the block as they walked, and his eyes grew wide when he spotted Mikey, the brother of the dude that killed Pretty Boy, walking in their direction.

DREAM ENTERED HER APARTMENT AND SLAMMED HER DOOR SHUT. "Stupid ass nigga," she grumbled, miserably displeased. Prince had definitely ruined her mood. She tossed her jacket on the couch then walked into her bathroom. As she peed, she thought about Prince and their relationship. She knew trying to change him and grow him up was a losing battle. Prince wasn't doing anything he didn't want to do until he felt like doing it. "Isn't that why I love his stubborn ass?" she asked herself as she wiped. Dream stood, pulled her sweats up, then washed her hands before making her way back over to her coat on the couch. She moved the stuffed envelope and frowned. "Where's Abby?" she questioned. If there was one thing Abby always did, it was wait up for her big sister, so she could get a percentage and knowledge.

Dream walked to Abby's room and opened the door, gasping at her discovery. "What are you doing?" she yelled. There, on Abby's bed, was Abby and Banko. In Banko's hand was a .38 revolver, and it was pointed at Abby's head. Abby giggled at her sister's terror. She was clearly gone off the E pills Banko had influenced her to take.

"Playing Russian Roulette," Abby replied, like it was nothing to play the dangerous game. It was a game that wasn't really a game. It was a suicide attempt. Dream dropped the envelope, causing dead presidents to spill all over the floor.

"Get the fuck out!" she yelled at Banko before running into her room. "I'm calling the fucking cops, so you need to leave now!" At the mention of the cops, Banko jumped up and quickly sobered up. He walked toward the door, but the sight of all that money on the floor stopped him in his tracks. He squatted down and began picking up the bills. "Put my shit down, you bum ass nigga!" The sound of Dream's voice caused him to jump. "Wait till I tell Prince!" she barked from the doorway. The threat set him off, and before he knew what he was doing, Banko rushed Dream and threw a punch as hard as Mayweather, causing her to crash into the entertainment system before falling to the floor with the flat screen television.

"Why would you do that!?" Abby yelled from behind him before running into her sister's room.

"Cause she think she the fucking shit! She think her nigga tough!" he spat, his face twisted in anger as he looked down at his swollen fist.

The impact from the punch had momentarily dazed Dream, and the fall had her body aching. Banko watched as she stood up, her nose leaking blood, and then pointed the gun at her, causing her eyes to grow to the size of golf balls.

"The fucking gun ain't loaded. I was just showing her how the game go. Look, you stupid bitch!" He pulled the trigger.

BOOM!

The loud blast caused them all to go temporarily deaf. Shock was plastered on their faces as Dream's hands went to the hole in the middle of her chest before she fell to the floor face first. Abby gasped in disbelief, hoping the ecstasy had her mind playing tricks on her. She prayed she was hallucinating. Her boyfriend holding a smoking gun. Her sister lying in a pool of her own blood. *This shit can't be real*, she told herself.

"The fuck did I do?" Banko whispered nervously. He turned to Abby, whose lips quivered and eyes misted. She looked like she was a nanosecond away from screaming. She slowly began walking toward Dream, but she was stopped by Banko's hand being wrapped around her throat so tightly that she couldn't breathe. "It was a mistake," he hissed as she looked at him, bewildered. "I'm sorry... I'm not going to jail for this shit." He placed the gun to her temple.

"THAT'S THE MIKEY NIGGA." PRINCE ALERTED HIS NIGGAS. BEFORE they could respond, Mikey could sense he was in danger. Prince took off in his direction, swinging as hard as he could. The punch landed on Mikey's jaw, and the force and surprise of it caused him to drop on top of a pile of snow, and before he knew it, he was kicked repeatedly. Blood covered his face as they stomped him out until he was barely conscious. Prince removed the gun from his waist and dug the barrel of it into Mikey's forehead. Mike-Mike and Kasper jumped back, and Money froze like he had stage fright. Kasper swiped his hand down his face nervously.

"Come on, bro. We gotta go before somebody sees us," he told Prince. All pleas fell on deaf ears, but the sound of the semi-automatic echoed through the quiet block and could be heard loud and clear as Prince pulled the trigger, sending a bullet through Mikey's skull.

BOOM!

Time seemed to stand still until Prince squeezed the trigger two more times. *BOOM! BOOM!* Like roaches when the lights came on, they took off in different directions. Prince ran as fast as he could enroute to Dream's house. It seemed like it took him forever, but the apartment was in view, and to his surprise, Money was close behind. They quickly made it to the apartment building and opened the door. "Woah!" Prince jumped back and pulled his gun. Mike-Mike raised his hands in fear.

"It's only me! Cuzzo, it's me!" Prince tried to calm his racing heart as they walked inside and locked the door behind them. Tears traveled down Mike-Mike's cheeks, and Money was on the verge of panicking as Prince sat down on the stairs silently.

"The-they locked... Kasper up," Mike-Mike stammered.

"What?" Prince looked up.

"We went to the train. That's how I got here so quick," Mike-Mike explained. "When I turned around, the Ds had him cuffed. Then, when I got here, I saw Banko running out, so I thought..." Mike-Mike stopped mid-sentence at the sound of sirens nearing. "Why would you kill him?"

"We had him put down," Money whispered. Prince looked at him and could see the fear in his eyes. He didn't want to have to kill Money too.

"My brother was murdered, nigga, not yours or yours," Prince replied seriously as the sirens stopped outside of the building. He stood, and they all stared at the door silently, unmoving and not knowing what to do. They jumped when the door handle jiggled, and they could hear the cops outside of the door attempting to gain entry. Mike-Mike began sobbing. "Shut the fuck up!" Prince told him as he grabbed him by his jacket. "Take the gun," he then told Money. "Go through the roof to the next building and get low. Get rid of it in the sewer," he instructed then handed the keys to his mother's crib to Money. "Don't tell anybody. Only us three and I know Kasper ain't no rat." Money grabbed both items and nodded his head in understanding.

"I love you, bro, and I got you!" he told Prince before running up to the roof with Mike-Mike close behind him.

Prince took two steps at a time, and to his surprise, Dream's apartment door was open. The putrid smell of blood and death was in the air, but Prince ignored it as he closed the door behind him and removed his jacket then walked into a situation that would change his life forever.

CHAPTER 1

July 07, 2020

Prince could hear the seven a.m. bell beginning to go off, announcing the institutional count and list. He laid on the flat state mattress, writing an email on his JP5 tablet and listening to music

Lil Durk featuring Lil Baby's *How I Know* played as he removed the KOSS headphones from his ears and sighed in frustration. He was tired of how he was allocating his time. Every morning, he would wake up at five in the morning, workout, do his hygiene, then write emails and listen to music until count time. When the bell rang, that was when his reality would set in. He was living in hell on Earth.

Eleven years… six months… twenty-one days… seven hours… one minute. That was how long it had been since the day Prince was detained and charged with the murder of Dream Cooper. Every night, he had nightmares about that fatal night. The nightmares were so consistent that he had barely slept in the eleven and a half years he had been incarcerated. That one night played in his head like the melody of his favorite song.

Prince noticed the scattered bills, and his brow dipped in confusion. He walked into Dream's room, and his heart sank like the Titanic. He rushed to Dream's side and tried to wake her up. When she wouldn't stir, he attempted CPR as he prayed for her to regain

consciousness, but it was too late. Prince immediately dug out his Blackberry and dialed 911. Tears welled in his eyes as he reported his finding, never minding the cops that were outside the building. He quickly hung up and stood up and ran to her sock drawer, retrieving his other gun. When he turned, he spotted Abby. She was sitting on the floor with her back against the wall in a state of shock. "Who did this?" he questioned her. Just then, revelation cut through him like a scalpel. He didn't need a verbal response. The look in Abby's eyes and him remembering Mike-Mike saying he saw Banko run out pointed the finger. Prince bit his inner jaw to stop the tears from spilling. Banko had murdered his bitch. Prince locked eyes with Abby as he held the gun in his hand and back peddled out the bedroom. They both knew what he was about to do. Why is she still breathing? Did she have a part in this? He stopped and thought as he contemplated killing Abby. Before he could decide, cops were running in with their weapons drawn. Prince and Abby never broke eye contact as he was roughly thrown to the ground and apprehended. A gun, Dream's blood on his clothes, his broken knuckle and her broken nose, plus the fact that he and Abby wouldn't utter a word was enough evidence for the jury to find him guilty of second-degree murder and for the judge to sentence him to nine years to life.

Due to his age, Prince was detained in a juvenile secure center where he would remain until he was twenty-one years old. But when it rained, it poured.

Four years into his bid, the NYPD announced the unsealing of two indictments charging a total of thirty-eight members and associates of Forever Famous and their opposition, a gang called Pimpset, with various robberies, assaults, and firearm offenses, including two gang related murders. What Prince didn't expect was for his name to be mentioned in the indictment. There had always been tension between the two teams since Pimpset was from the same block the nigga who killed Pretty Boy was from, and they rocked with his little brother, but it became murder beef when Prince killed Mikey, who was one of the leaders. After being rearrested and charged with Mikey's murder, he was transferred to Rikers Island due to being nineteen at the time. Money was his co-defendant and the reason they even knew about the murder. One night, he had run his mouth to another member of Forever Famous named Josh. A few weeks later, Josh was arrested for several burglaries and a gun charge and told the district attorney what he knew. For two years, Prince sat on Rikers Island amongst twenty of his day ones, fighting cases and opps. Although they had made his life worse, he was happy to be around his niggas and solidified his position as head of the gang.

Forever Famous had grown in numbers, and Money, Sport, and Kelz had established them while Prince was gone. They were his three headed goat. It wasn't until niggas got sentenced, went home, and he was sent upstate with six extra years that he realized that everybody wasn't who they said they were or who they pretended to be. That was when the hate for them grew. Prince shook his head, and his body filled with rage at the reality of his circumstances. The routine had long ago become redundant, and he yearned for the day that he was able to do what he wanted, when he wanted to do it. He had been incarcerated for so long that he hadn't been able to explore and experience most things that he found interesting because he missed out on a man's most adventurous years. The fucked-up part was that he would probably never get a chance. His thoughts went to Banko.

"Bitch ass nigga," Prince mumbled, balling up his fist. He had never even thought about whispering Benko's name, and in return, Banko never sent him a penny, a picture, a message, not even his respect. Banko wasn't the only one either. Mike-Mike had never reached out either, and it had been more than five years since he last spoke to Kasper. Neither one of them had gotten caught up in the indictment, and both were in their own worlds. But they would have to answer for the slight one day.

At the beginning, Abby would send pictures and money orders consistently, but words were never exchanged between the two. Prince's inmate's account was stacked because of her, but it had been years since she sent anything as well – ever since he was re-sentenced. Abby knew the real from the case, but from what Prince heard, the bitch had been out there throwing dirt on his name. Prince felt like everybody had counted him out. He just hoped they kept the same energy. It was crazy how the people who he would die for wouldn't even ride for him. The last few years had frozen his cold heart. Prince had been to some of the worst prisons, and each had made him worse. Attica, Clinton, Auburn, Great Meadow, Elmira, Wende, he had run through those fields and had brushed shoulders with men who were well known murderers, master manipulators, and his big homies. On top of that, he had been gangbanging, so he didn't just witness the savagery. He had experienced it as well. All of the slashings, stabbings, riots, and prison politics robbed him of any innocence he might have had left. The fourteen-year-old pretty boy with a quick trigger finger was now a twenty-six-year-old demon.

Prince was now five foot eleven and weighed one hundred seventy pounds solid. His arms and chest were cut up and covered in tattoos, causing his body to resemble a brick wall decorated with graffiti. His once clean-shaven, baby face was now ruggedly handsome with a full beard. Physically, Prince was what bitches wanted; mentally, he was what niggas weren't ready for.

"Smith, are you coming out for porter?" C.O. Marshall asked as he stopped in front of Prince's cell, count sheet in his hand. Prince nodded in response. A porter was an assigned inmate who came out while the rest of the tier was locked in. They cleaned, handed out water and supplies, and basically ran the whole company. Everybody wanted to be a porter in order to have extra time roaming the tier; Prince used the job to support his hustle. Prison was like the streets, and everybody had a vice. Weed, dope, pills, every drug was sold in prison for a good price. Prince's vice was the money. He had never sold drugs in the streets or understood hand to hand operations, but after seeing the money drugs made in prison and the power it contained, hustling became his occupation. It turned out he had a niche for running it up and running shit. Prince quickly dressed in red joggers, a white t-shirt, and red Jordan11s then put on a pair of latex gloves and a face mask.

The United States of America was in the crisis of the coronavirus, also known as the Covid-19 pandemic, and bodies were dropping like beats. Governor Cuomo had declared a disaster emergency in the state of New York in response to the outbreak. Although the virus was slowly subsiding, the death toll in the country had reached six hundred thousand, and New York was the epicenter of the U.S. Covid-19 public health crisis. Vaccination was mandated for certain occupations and offered to everyone, including incarcerated individuals. Prince had refused to take a vaccine but took all precautions. *I refuse to die before I can flex on everybody that left me for dead*, he thought as his cell gate cracked open. Grabbing his tablet, he walked out of his cell, heading down the tier.

"Top of the morning. Top of the red." Several voices could be heard yelling out their daily greetings and salutations as he entered the slop sink and began filling up the water barrow in order to pour water into the buckets of the inmates in the tier. As it filled, Prince logged onto the kiosk and connected his tablet. This was how inmates sent and received emails and video grams and purchased music, movies, and games. After syncing his tablet, he unplugged it, grabbed the water barrow, and pushed it up the tier.

"Yo, Prince, top of the morning, bro." A white dude named B. Lo spoke as Prince poured water in his bucket.

"Niggas only call someone big bro when they want something. What you want?" Prince replied. B. Lo was a fiend who would sell his or his mother's soul for drugs.

A lot of dudes in prison would, and Prince was the devil that would buy them. "That $150 gonna be done today. Can I get another strip to make it an even $200?" B. Lo asked. K2 and Suboxone strips were two drugs that were highly addictive and requested in prison, and luckily, Prince had a plug for them both. "That's my word..."

"Na, that's your ass if my $200 not there by the end of one o'clock rec." Prince cut him off while he dug inside his boxer briefs and removed a gloved finger containing the drugs. He removed an orange strip that resembled a Listerine strip and handed it to B. Lo before moving up the tier. "Super loyal, bro." Prince saluted as he stopped in front of thirty-two cell.

F.L. looked up from the breakfast he was preparing. "That's over royalty, my guy. What the vibe, friggity?"

Prince had met thousands of motherfuckers over the years he'd been incarcerated. Most were burdens, some were beneficial, and a few were bros. F.L. was his brother. Their bond had started due to their affiliation. A mutual vision had solidified that bond, and after seeing through the indoctrination of their affiliate, they had cut ties together and were building something of their own. They were two niggas on the same mission with a desire for the same things – money, bitches, and fame.

"Regular shit, bro," Prince replied as he unlocked his tablet and began scrolling through his emails. "I'm still waiting on Sport to link shorty for tomorrow. I'm fake getting low," he said, referring to drugs.

"My young boy putting something together too, so bro just gotta link him before he link her type shit," F.L. said. Visits had only been reopened for two weeks after being shut down due to Covid-19, so they were playing catch up with the money. "Niggas need a line on that paper plane," F.L. told him. Paper plane was the new wave, cotton paper soaked with the same chemicals used to enhance K2. The get back for one page was crazy, and Prince wanted parts.

"I got niggas on that too. You know my body. I'm on every money wave." He paused to read an email. "Shorty said Sport still ain't answer her. Bro blowing mines, no funny shit," Prince said. Over the years, things had changed dramatically. Out of sight, out of mind was apparent. Females came and went, family were sometimers, and niggas played games they normally wouldn't play.

There were only a handful that stood a hunnit, and those were the ones he would give Heaven on Earth. *I'ma make sure little mama good until my last breath...* He thought about the female whose face he had tatted on his arm.

"Niggas gonna fall in line if that reversal fall through," F.L. said, breaking Prince out of his thoughts. A few months before the pandemic, Prince, F.L., and a law library clerk had looked over Prince's transcripts and found several loopholes. It was shit Prince had never noticed because he was so distracted by jailhouse bullshit. It wasn't until he lost somebody that motivated him that he began to think outside the walls. He had goals that could only be achieved if he made it out. Although he didn't believe in the justice system, they had helped him submit a motion to vacate his sentence, and if granted, he would be immediately released. Now that the courts were back in motion, time was ticking, and the district attorney only had four days to answer.

"Whatever happens happens," Prince replied.

F.L. looked at him like he had two heads. He kept his thoughts to himself, but he had been peeping how Prince seemed to have lost hope of making it home. "Fuck you mean? Bro, there's too much shit that was overlooked. Shorty was killed by a bullet of a .38, but you were caught with a .40 that was never shot. Then, the time of death of your manslaughter is two minutes before her time of death, which makes it impossible for you to have killed two people who were damn near ten blocks away from each other. The only witness never said that you did anything, and you were the 911 caller."

"Let's not forget my hand was broken, and her nose was, so they think I hit her, and let's not forget they knew all this shit at my trial," Prince stated.

"The gunpowder was from the first murder, and the body was beaten before he was shot. They ain't know about that one at trial. Your lawyer was ineffective for not getting you an appeal after this came out in the last case. But right now, with all this prison reform and newly discovered evidence, bro, you'll be home by the end of the summer, nigga," F.L. said surely before he paused. "And real shit, I respect the fact you never told me who did it or that you won't mention that shorty sister was supporting you after everything. I know you ain't letting shit go once you do get there. All I'm saying is this, bro. You had clout already. Nigga, you you. But shit gonna be real different, and you don't need to come back here, bro. This shit we doing could be epic."

"I don't expect to make it. That's just me being real with myself," Prince told him. "But if I do, I'ma terrorize."

"I got fifty years, bro. I need you out there cause I know a real nigga never gonna fold or forget about me," F.L. responded.

"If I make it, I got you, bro," Prince promised. "But son, they took all these years from me, and motherfuckers who shitted on me made me worse. I can't let that rock, bro."

F.L. felt for his nigga. "You gonna make it."

Elmira Correctional Facility was classified as a maximum-security prison and was considered one of the worst in the state of New York. The prison housed approximately twelve hundred inmates and had some of the most corrupt correctional officers. Prince and F.L. walked through the metal detectors enroute to the fieldhouses where recreation was held. Prince's head was on a swivel as he inconspicuously gripped a black ceramic scalpel in his right hand. They entered the fieldhouse and walked into the phone cage where twenty-six phones lined the wall. Each phone was labeled by different organizations. The Bloods, the upstate dudes, the Muslims, and the Brooklyn boys all had their own two or three phones. Prince nodded and dapped a few people he knew before getting on a phone near a comrade. "S.L., bro." He spoke to the twenty-year-old white boy.

"You know the vibes, big bro," Designer replied. "I just pushed that bread to you too." Designer was Prince's young boy. They had met while being cellmates in the box, and Prince had taken a liking to him. Designer had proved himself plenty of times, and for that, he had become family. If Prince was getting money, he made sure Designer was too.

"I'ma sturdy you up tomorrow," Prince told him as he dialed his din number then a phone number.

"Baeee…" Mia cooed into the phone upon accepting the call. "I was just thinking about you."

Prince had met Mia a few months prior. She was the friend of a female acquaintance who linked the two. After a few phone conversations, Mia had visited and quickly tried to stake her claim. They had been rocking for months, and although she wasn't who he wanted, Prince fucked with shorty. Baby was a rider. Mia was twenty-seven years old and had a few things going for herself. She was a guidance counselor at a public school, had no kids or habits, and looked good enough to eat.

"That's regular shit," he replied cockily, causing her to giggle. "Any money get there?" he asked, wondering why the fuck B. Lo was walking around the track instead of on the phone taking care of his business.

"You're something else and yeah," Mia paused. "R.S. sent $150, Breeze sent $200, $50 from Tana, and Designer just sent $350, plus you already got $1,650 on the Cash App," she informed. Prince smirked. $2400 was nothing. But for a nigga in his circumstances to be making that, sometimes weekly, it was everything and represented his independence. "Anyway, Mister… I miss you and can't wait to see you tomorrow. I got your food package, and if you need anything else, let me know now," Mia told him.

"I'm good. I appreciate you. Sport hit you yet?" he asked.

"He actually did! He had lost that phone, so he gave me the new number for you," Mia said. Relief washed over Prince. He had thought Sport was moving wocky.

"Call him," he insisted.

"Yooo, gang." A voice came through the receiver after a brief silence.

"Fuck is the vibes, bro? How you?" Prince asked.

"Everything good, my nigga. I had lost my jack, but I'm back like I never left. Talk to me, my boy," Sport responded. Sport was a day one. He had been there since Forever Famous was started and had done four years due to the indictment.

"I need a line on some guss, bro. You know my body. We ain't gotta talk too much," Prince told him.

A thought came to Sport's mind. "Bro, I got a cash cow as we speak!" He grew excited. "When sis pulling up on you?"

"Tomorrow," Prince answered.

"Tell her slide on me first so…" Sport started, but Prince interrupted.

"Na, you slide with her, nigga," Prince said. "It's been a minute. You come tell me the vibes."

"Say less, bro. I'ma be there. That's gangsta!" Sport swore. "I'ma hit sis after we hang up." They spoke for a few more minutes then hung up.

As soon as they did, Mia started her shit. "I don't even know why you depending on him or why you didn't ask me if I was okay with him coming with me," she complained.

"He tryna talk money. You tryna beef. Make sure he pull up. If you don't want to, I'll see you when you decide that you do." He hung up before she could respond. His next call was to Money.

"What's the vibe, gang? S.L.!" Money quickly answered.

After doing his six-year bid, Money had gone home and played the cut. But whenever Prince needed him, he was on the front line. He was really the only person Prince could depend on and one of the first people Prince told about the move him and F.L. were putting together.

"You healthy?"

"Over royalty."

"Hell yeah, bro. What you fucking with?" Prince could hear noise in the background.

"At Kelz crib, bout to leave and get ready for work. I get my check tonight, so I'ma have a few dollars for you."

"Heard, bro. Wassup with Bentley bitch ass?" Prince asked. Like Designer, Prince had met Bentley while being cellmates in the box and had situated him when he got home. Unlike Designer, Bentley was a certified fuck up.

"Son a joker. He's out here, but he ain't really on shit," Money informed. "I'ma text him now. Hold up, bro."

"Hey, light skin." A soft voice came through the phone.

"Who this?" Prince asked, confused. The voice was soft and sexy but unfamiliar.

"Your future baby mother. How you don't remember me?"

"A nigga been through so much that all I remember is the bad," Prince said sadly and honestly.

"Nigga, you ain't hear? I am the bad," she said salaciously. "This is Lani."

CHAPTER 2

Gunboy's eyes took in the scene as he leaned against the handball court, chewing on his inner jaw. He scoffed as he listened to the preaching going on. *Niggas lucky I ain't grippy right now*, he thought angrily.

"Chill, bro," Kelz whispered to him. They were partners in crime, and he had learned to pick up on Gunboy's moods. In his seventeen years of living, Gunboy had never bit his tongue for anybody. He was the youngest in the regime and had earned his respect and right to vote on a decision. Most of the members had been affiliated before he was off the porch, but he was sure he had put in just as much if not more. Kelz had brought him into the family, and there wasn't too many niggas drilling like him. His five foot, one hundred forty-pound frame and yellow skin, long hair, and baby face wasn't intimidating at all. It was his name and resume that kept niggas cautious.

"This shit pointless as fuck," Gunboy spoke, interrupting the preaching. Those who knew him had been waiting for this. Everybody turned their head in his direction as he came off the wall, hands moving animatedly. "Cause I ain't squashing shit, and I damn sure ain't shaking hands."

"Boy, you dead ass right now!" the six-six, three hundred plus pound preacher snapped. "Grow the fuck up! Nigga, I'm the one running this shit!" His name was House. He had been one of the original members, and while everybody was fighting cases, he kept them relevant in the streets and took the front seat. Gunboy's laughter cut him off.

"Niggas done died for this shit and did time. How the fuck you talking this togetherness shit wit these bitch ass niggas?"

"Boy, you's a baby. This ain't really what you want," Booga responded, grilling Gunboy callously. Booga Bread had always been a main factor in Pimpset, and like House, he had sidestepped the indictment and had taken over. Booga had glowed up, and his name sounded like something all through the borough. He had recreated and renamed Pimpset. Nowadays, they were known as Team Self Made, and they had the streets in a chokehold. Booga and House had been getting a few dollars together and since they both were leading had decided to let bygones be bygones.

"Nigga, you's a bitch," Gunboy spat back, unimpressed with Booga's resume. He moved forward at the same time that Booga did, but they were both stopped before they could reach each other. "You know my body, nigga! I'm a demon! Gunboy gonna drill. It's a name and warning, nigga!" he barked back as Kelz pushed him out of the gate of the handball courts.

"I would hurt that little nigga," House said angrily. He had ensured Booga that everybody would be onboard. Only seven blocks separated the two teams, and that was making it hard to get money in the hood.

Sport walked into the gates, looking around. He eyed the opps and shook his head. "You should of knew some bullshit was going to happen," he told House as he approached. "You should of at least hollered before you did this dumb shit. I don't know why Prince got you driving." He shook his head again before walking out. Prince was the head, House was the face, Kelz and Money were the brains, but Sport was the body. Gunboy and everybody drilled, but Sport killed, and even the opps hesitated with him. Sport had his own tricks up his sleeve, and before anybody could try to figure them out, it would be too late.

"He gonna call back?" Lani asked, her lips poking out in a pout before pulling on the blunt that was between her fingertips.

Money couldn't help but laugh." You on his heels!" he joked as he sat on the couch next to Lani, one foot resting on the coffee table as he leaned back, staring through the weed smoke at the ceiling. His thoughts always ran rampant when he spoke to Prince. The long hours in the interrogation room had broken Money. Or was it the threat of life imprisonment that caused him to sign the statement indicating that he passed Prince a gun and watched as Prince shot Mikey? He had later tried to recant the false statement, but it was already too late, and the damage was already done. Luckily for him, Prince had kept the dishonor a secret and still allowed Money to reap the benefits of a stand-up individual. Ever since they were young, Prince had been saving him and sparing him, leading while he followed. Money had been home about a year and was expecting his first child. He worked overnight at Rite Aid and was barely on the scene. His thoughts and plans had been desultory for a while when it came to his involvement with F.F. On one hand, he knew he had to let go and prepare for his child to be born, but on the other hand, he loved it too much and loved the power, fame, and resources that were at his fingertips because of it. Every time he spoke to Prince, he felt like he had to prove himself and play his part, like he had to take the lead and level the gang up, especially with the new direction Prince wanted to take them.

I could clean that blemish... he thought. He ran a hand down his head and blew out a sharp breath. Lani giggled joyously, her chinky eyes even lower, confirming that she was high.

"I look good good, nigga. Imagine me on a nigga heels," she said, taking another pull. Truth was, she had been crushing on Prince since she was young. Back then, she was a nobody with no body. She was nerdy with no sense of fashion, and nobody would look her way. Oh, how times had changed. After Dream was murdered, Abby had stepped into her Red Bottoms and took off, scamming with the knowledge Dream had given her. Unfortunately, she was stumbling, lacking the brains of the finesse. So, she recruited the smartest girl she knew, Lani. Lani was invested in her profession – a degree in accounting, a job at the bank. She had all the tools she needed to keep her pieces hitting, and since they were, she had everything she had ever wanted. The condominium in Toms Rivers, New Jersey, the 2020 Mercedes Benz GT 63 S, a laundromat, and the body women would die for. The nobody with no body was a baddie with a new ass and new titties that she purchased in Colombia. Lani was now a ten, and her confidence was on a hundred. She was five feet two inches of perfection with a slim waist, ass the size of two NBA basketballs, perky 36DD breasts, a toned stomach, and drip that had motherfuckers on her body like skin. She had light skin, black, silky hair that fell down to the middle of her back, and bright eyes the color of silver. The full sleeve on her left arm was a work of art, and the tattoos under her breasts and down her right ribs proved she could take a little pain. The same niggas and bitches that used to laugh at her, she flexed on regularly. Lani treated niggas like bitches and let bitches know they couldn't compete. Only a handful had the privilege to sample her sex, and she was okay with that. Lani wasn't pressed for any nigga, but Prince was interesting to her. "Next time ya speak, give him my number," Lani told Money. She knew she was pushing it. Abby was her best friend, and Prince was locked up for killing her sister. Lani couldn't possibly talk to him, right? *Wrong...* she thought to herself. Lani knew things most people didn't.

Money chuckled this time. Lani was a piece of work. She was what Dream would have been, and Money had no doubt that Prince would snatch her up, especially for the flex. But Money needed her to solidify his position. On top of that, he had been wanting to fuck Lani for a while now, but she wouldn't let him exit the friend zone. "I'ma see wassup. But yo…"

"Why you say it like it's something wrong with that?" Lani cut him off. "Hope it ain't cause of that basic bitch, Mia." She scrunched her nose up as she put out the blunt.

"Nothing wrong with that but bro invested in ol' girl. But listen, I need you to put me on," Money responded, feeling like a whack nigga.

Lani peeped the salt but ignored it. "Put you on how?" She gave him the side-eye. Money was like family, and they had been cool since Kelz started fucking with Lani's stepsister, but she was very selective with who she dealt with on a business level, and there was something about him Lani didn't trust. Niggas didn't want to hustle their way up. They wanted the easy way, and never would she give up her sauce or risk fucking up her grind. She had too much to lose.

"I need a kitchen and sauce," Money said, going for it all.

He could of said some bins, some accounts. This nigga want the whole sitchy, Lani said to herself. This was why she would never put him on. Money was more of a drug dealer than a scammer. "I can't do that. But if you need a few dollars, then you know…"

Before she could finish her sentence, the front door opened then slammed. They both looked up, brows dipped at Nicole's hasty movement and noticeable anxiousness. "What's wrong?" They watched as Nicole sat on the coffee table directly in front of them and removed a plastic bag from her purse before turning the bag upside down and spilling the contents in Money's lap.

"Where's Kelz?"

"Woah!" Lani exclaimed, eyeing the stacks of money. The money didn't move her. Her bag was high fashion. It was the fact that her sister, the one who wanted no parts of the illegality, had just came home from her nine to five at a car rental spot and dropped what looked like $20,000 on Money's lap. Money's eyes went wide as he stared at the dead faces then locked eyes with Nicole.

"Where the fuck you get this?"

"Chow!" the C.O. yelled as he pulled the levers to open cells for dinner. Prince walked out, closing his cell behind him, then took hurried steps off the company. He had told B. Lo what the consequences would be if he didn't send the money he owed. Now, Prince was taking it in blood.

"You walking with a purpose. Who did it, bro, so I could set they ass on fire?" Designer said as he caught up with Prince at the bottom of the steps.

"I'll holla when we get to the mess hall," Prince told him as they stood on the bottom tier, waiting on the escort C.O. to let the company walk out. They walked outside and hurried enroute to the mess hall. They entered the mess hall, giving head nods to a few people and walking the chow line. "B. Lo shot," Prince told Designer as they grabbed trays. "So, I'ma clap him." Designer shrugged. No explanation was needed. If Prince played Steve Kerr, Designer was Stephen Curry. "Na," Prince said as they sat at a table. "I guess niggas think I lost it or something. My money getting played with, so I'ma show boy my gun still go off."

They waited patiently until it was time to go then stood to leave. B. Lo walked in front of them, engaged in a deep conversation with another white boy. Prince waited until they were outside and in a large group before he removed the scalpel from his mouth and closed the gap between him and B. Lo. Prince swiftly reached past B. Lo's face then pressed the weapon into his flesh, applied pressure, and yanked back, ripping B. Lo's face from nose to ear before pushing past him and moving to the front of the group.

"Ah! Fuck, man!" B. Lo yelled out, alerting the C.O.s. Blood poured from the laceration as he pressed his hand to his face.

"Move! Move! Everybody on the ground!" the escorting C.O. yelled as he pressed the body alarm. "On the fucking ground now!"

"LET ME SEE YOUR KEYS," GUNBOY SAID AS HE SAT UP FROM BETWEEN the thick creamy thighs he had been lying on.

"My keys for what?" His girlfriend, Mikayla, frowned and put her phone down. Mikayla was a good girl. She was an eighteen-year-old freshman at LaGuardia College who kept her nose clean. She was beautiful inside and out with her calm personality, pale skin, and pretty brown eyes. Mikayla had black, shoulder length hair that she kept bone straight, was thick from the waist down, and had cantaloupe sized breasts. She had been in an on again off again relationship with Gunboy since middle school and couldn't seem to let him go. "I thought you was staying?"

"I am. I'm bouta grab some food," he explained as he stood and stretched. The blunt he had blown with Kelz had left him with the munchies. "Get your ass up." He kicked the loveseat where Kelz was slumped, snoring lightly. Gunboy laughed when Kelz didn't even stir. "I'ma run to McDonald's," he told Mikayla. Mikayla sighed then stood and walked to the back to grab her keys. Gunboy quickly lifted the cushion of the couch and reached for his gun.

"Absolutely not!" Mikayla sneered, her arms folded across her chest as she stared a hole through Gunboy. "You're not driving my car with a gun on you!"

"Bro, don't start." Gunboy swiped a hand down his face as he blew out a breath of exasperation. He knew how she felt about his lifestyle. She wouldn't berate him for it, but she asked that he never put her in jeopardy or in the mix. Mikayla was too naive to realize that she was a target from the many times she posted him on her social media. "Just give me the keys."

"Don't call me bro!" she barked, a frown on her pretty face. "Leave the gun, Xavier," she stated firmly, using his government name.

Gunboy threw the gun on the couch then snatched the keys from her hand and stormed out. The drive to McDonald's was less than ten minutes, and his stomach growled in appreciation when he walked inside and smelled the greasy fast food. *Fuck I didn't go through the drive thru?* he chastised himself, shaking his head. Gunboy hated drive thrus, because they always seemed to forget some shit, but right now, he regretted walking inside. This was the closest McDonald's but the most ghetto one in the hood. It was packed and moving at a snail's pace since the only working register was being worked by a brown skinned female who was engaged in a conversation with some guy. "Fuck, yo!" He shook his head. There was about five people between him and the dude.

"I know, right?" the pretty, petite female who stood in front of him commented, looking back at him. She was beautiful, and if he wasn't so hungry, he would have engaged. They locked eyes and gave each other a tight smile.

"Watch this," he told her. "Yo, nigga!" Gunboy said as he walked past the other five customers. "You holding up the fucking line."

The dude's face twisted in confusion as he turned to Gunboy. "What?" he grilled.

"Uh-unn." The girl at the register, Kimmy, tried to stop the situation before it could even start. Unlike August, she knew who Gunboy was and the rumors surrounding his name. But she also knew how August, her ex-boyfriend, gave it up. He had just returned from down south after ten years and hadn't changed a bit.

"Un-unh what?" Gunboy asked, fuming. "You better let this bitch nigga know, Kimmy."

"Bitch nigga?" August spat. "You know this nigga?" he asked, looking from Gunboy to Kimmy and back as his hand went to his hip, grabbing and displaying the butt of his gun. Gunboy chuckled, lifting his hands in surrender as he back peddled, putting distance between them as August attempted to withdraw. Kimmy quickly reached over the counter, stopping him, but the damage was already done. Gunboy's body filled with anger as he pushed out the entrance and rushed to the car before he pulled off. He pulled in front of Mikayla's building and didn't even realize the door was locked. "Kayla... Kayla!" he yelled.

"Why are you screaming like..." Mikayla said, sticking her head out the window.

"Bitch, get my fucking gun! Go get my shit right now!" Gunboy barked, cutting her off.

Mikayla's eyes grew wide. He had never called her out her name, and the look on his face told her now wasn't the time to argue. She ran to the couch and shook Kelz awake. "Something-Something happened," she stuttered scarily. "He's downstairs and wants his gun."

Kelz shook off his sleep and quickly jumped up. He grabbed the gun from the couch where Gunboy had thrown it and raced out the door and down the stairs. He walked outside to find Gunboy pacing back-and-forth on the sidewalk. "Fuck happened?"

Gunboy grabbed the gun from Kelz as he turned toward the car. "Nigga backed me down." There was nothing else to talk about.

"Say that," Kelz said as his anger grew. Gunboy was a trouble-maker, but right or wrong, that was his baby boy. Kelz texted as they swerved into the McDonald's parking lot. The big windows made it easy to spot August. "Boy in there?" Kelz said as they sat, waiting for him to come out.

"Yup," Gunboy replied before opening the driver's door and getting out as August was exiting with a few other people close by. Gunboy wasted no time and had no sympathy for innocent bystanders as he moved toward the entrance, lifted his pistol, and squeezed the trigger as he tried his hardest to annihilate August. Everybody dropped to the ground as Gunboy ran back to the car and sped off, leaving blood on the pavement and one clinging to their life.

———

"IT IS WHAT IT IS LIKE DRAKE SAID, MY NIGGA," SPORT RESPONDED TO the person he was talking to on the phone as he opened the door. He smiled at Mia as he let her in. He couldn't help watching her ass move in her jeans as she walked in. "I'll let niggas know the play tomorrow," he said as he closed the door. "Iight, bet." He hung up then walked into the living room. "Sup, Ma?"

"Sup, bro?" Mia smiled at Sport as she sat on his couch. "I figured since you live closer, we could just leave from here. Plus, I still have to put the shit together, and I didn't get no sleep, soooooo…" she stated as she watched him grab two ounces of weed from his cabinet and place it on the coffee table. "Please tell me you got Saran Wrap or gloves," she said as she dumped the weed out of the Ziploc bag.

"Probably some gloves," Sport told her as he sat on the arm of the couch, watching her. "He lucky to have you. For real." He got up then returned with a box of latex gloves.

"Thank you," Mia told him as she began putting shit together. They talked and laughed as she did, and before they knew it, two hours had passed. Mia looked at her phone for the hundredth time and exhaled.

"You good?" Sport asked as he sat next to her, watching *SportsCenter*.

"I'm just wondering why the fuck my man ain't call me yet." She bit her bottom lip.

Sport chuckled. "Don't stress that. You want a drink?" He got up and grabbed two cups and a bottle of Hennessy. "He probably vibing right now, might as well do the same," he said slickly. Mia was Prince's girl and all, but it was what it was, and Sport wanted what he wanted. He had his eyes on the throne and everything that came with it.

Mia rolled her eyes and grabbed a cup. "He ain't stupid."

Sport laughed. "Hope you ain't stupid."

Mia frowned in confusion. "What you mean by that?"

CHAPTER 3

S in yawned as he descended the stairs and scanned the block. At one in the morning, the slight summer night breeze felt good, but he was too tired to appreciate it. Sin lived a vampire life. He slept during the day and grinded during the night because it was when his trap phone blinged the most. Sin's clientele was profitable, and his phone was worth some shit to anybody who got their hands on it. It had been passed down to him by his uncle when he was sent to the Feds, and ever since then, Sin glowed up.

Sin turned the corner and bumped into Gloria, Nana's mother. "What you doing out so late?" He hugged her.

Gloria kissed his cheeks. "I'm grown, little boy, and I'm on my way to work. What your ass doing out so late?" Gloria asked. She had watched them all grow from bad ass boys to men and was well aware of the stories told about them. Nana was her only child, so instead of pushing him away by disapproving of his friends, she embraced them and dotted on them motherly.

Sin gave a slight smile. "You know what it is, Ma. I'm just coming out," he informed as he eyed her in her security uniform. Everybody knew Gloria was sexy. She was a caramel Puerto Rican with a slight accent, long, black hair, and thick thighs. But she was off limits.

"Un-unh." She shook her head before squinting her eyes and looking past Sin. "Who the hell is that?"

She watched as two guys suspiciously crossed the street, heading in their direction. Sin looked in the direction that she nodded toward and was glad he did. One guy looked around as the other reached under his shirt. The face masks they wore couldn't hide their identities from Sin. He quickly turned and ran inside the chicken spot. "Move! Move!" he yelled, pushing past the three customers as the first shot rang out. *BOOM!* Sin ducked as he ran under the partition of the counter. *BOOM! BOOM! BOOM!* He could hear screams and cries as he pushed open the back door and climbed the gate. Sin had a good relationship with the owners of the chicken spot, and luckily, their backyard connected with the backyard of the building he hustled out of. He climbed the fire escape until he made it to the roof then sat with his back against the roof door, catching his breath. Chucky and London were both a part of Team Self Made, so it wasn't surprising that they threw shots. He just couldn't understand why now when they had crossed paths plenty of times and kept it cordial. Sin had a feeling it had something to do with the several missed calls and unread text messages he had.

Mia looked at the time on the clock, and regret hit her like a truck. It was already two in the morning, and they should have been getting ready to leave so that they'd be on time for the visit. If she missed it, it would be the first one she missed, and she knew she was dead wrong. Her forehead pinched as Sport pulled her clit in between his lips and sucked. She moaned out and arched her back. She blamed it on the Henny. They had been drinking as she bagged up, and the next thing she knew, she was lying down on the couch, and her jeans and panties were on the floor. Sport had been eating her pussy for hours, and she had cum more times than she could count. With each orgasm, her guilt faded. Her clit was sore and sensitive, but Mia couldn't get enough of his head game. It had been close to a year since she had been intimate, so the more he made her pussy cum, the more she wanted him to continue the pleasure. But he was Prince's friend, and they were supposed to be on their way to visit him.

"Okay. Okay. Okay. Stop!" She moaned as Sport pushed his tongue as deep as he could. It was like he couldn't get enough of the taste of her juices. Mia placed her hand on his forehead to push him away, but when he swirled his tongue inside her, her hand made its way to the back of his head, forcing him deeper.

Her mind played Ping Pong with her body, and at the moment, Mia's body was winning.

Sport kissed up her body as Mia's phone alerted. Something forced her to turn her head and look at her screen, and she could see that it was a notification from the Jpay app. It was an email from Prince. She gasped as she pushed Sport away. "I can't do him like this," she told him as she stood up and ran to the bathroom. Mia rushed in and closed then locked the door behind her before sitting down on the toilet and running her hands through her wild hair. The guilt was now eating at her. The email had to be sent earlier, so for her to have gotten it now was a sign. "I gotta get out of here." She sniffled "I gotta go see him. What did I do?"

She stood up and opened the door, only to find Sport standing naked. "If you want to leave, I respect it, Ma. But this between me and you if you wanna stay," Sport told her. "Son not here, and if he was, he'll be doing him too."

THE SOUND OF RUSHED FOOTSTEPS CAUSED PRINCE TO SIT UP ON HIS bed. A CO made rounds every thirty minutes during the night tour, but this sounded like a bunch, and it sounded like they were on a mission. The footsteps came to a halt in front of his cell, and the blanket he had covering his cell was snatched. "Smith, turn your light on for me and stand at your gate," a sergeant demanded.

"For what?" Prince asked as he stood up. It was two a.m. Any movement should have been restricted at this time.

"I'll answer your questions when we move you," the sergeant

responded as four COs stood behind him, one of them removing handcuffs from his belt.

Prince turned on his light before placing his sneakers on his feet. "Where am I being moved to at two in the morning?" he asked. Correctional officers were known for killing inmates in state prisons. Over the years, Prince had heard the rumors about an inmate being taken out of his cell and disappearing.

"Again, I'll answer…"

Prince quickly cut him off. "Listen, I don't feel safe leaving my cell at this time of night. That's not…"

"It's happening one way or another," the CO holding the handcuffs said. "Cuff up and let us move you."

"Come in here and cuff me," Prince replied seriously. "Like I said, Sarge, I wanna know where I'm going and why."

"Yo, you good, bro?" his neighbor, N. Dot, asked. "What's up, Sergeant Petri? What ya tryna do with him?" he asked loudly, causing other inmates to wake up, inquiring and talking shit to the COs.

"Listen," Sergeant Petri lowered his voice and moved closer to Prince's gate, "the outside camera shows that you cut the guy earlier. I was told to strip and frisk you, and if nothing is found, you'll be moving to I block."

Prince turned and allowed them to handcuff him, mentally kicking himself in the ass. He had actually cut B. Lo for no reason. Mia had sent him an email telling him B. Lo's $200 had gotten there, but it was already too late. Now, because of that, he was being moved, most likely to the box.

"If I'm moving to the box, just say that," Prince told the sergeant as his cell opened.

"If we find anything you're not supposed to have, then you are. If not, then you not," the sergeant replied.

Prince watched as three COs went inside his cell and began to search. He had to bite the inside of his jaw to keep his composure as they tore his cell up. They stepped on food, threw clothes on the floor, ripped papers, everything they could do to get a reaction from him. After they were done, they packed up his things, and Prince was moved to I block and placed in another cell then strip frisked before they left.

"Yoo, twelve cell, what's your handle?" his neighbor knocked on the wall and asked.

Prince hated being moved to new blocks. He knew a few people on I block, but since the prison was kind of segregated, he didn't know who else was in the cut. He had a list of enemies and didn't want to put them on point if they were nearby. "I'll tell you when the cells open," Prince responded as he sat on the bed. He had a visit in the morning, but there was no way he was getting any sleep tonight.

Morning came fast, and before Prince knew it, the count bell was going off. He had been up all night, preparing himself for whatever was to come. He hadn't even unpacked his property. He had been sharpening a knife all night. If a nigga played, fuck cutting his face, Prince was taking his life. He sat silently, listening to see if there was a familiar face. When the porter stopped at his cell, Prince couldn't help but to smile. "My motherfucking nigga!"

Drop.b leaned in. "I thought that was you last night. I just didn't wanna shout you out like that." He dapped Prince. Prince and Drop.b had been good friends for ten plus years, since being in a juvenile center together. Drop.b was a solid dude.

"Yeah, they moved me for booming something. Who over here?" Prince asked.

"Few niggas. Nobody special tho. Why? You sturdy, bro?" Drop.b asked.

"You know my body, always on offense, bro," Prince told him.

"Of course. It's money over here tho. I been tryna get next to you for a minute. Now, we could put something together," Drop.b said. "Let me do this water, and I'ma pull back up on you."

Prince nodded. "Say that, bro. I'm waiting on a visit now. So, I'ma be on deck with it."

"Say less, my guy." Drop.b walked away.

Prince began going through his bags, removing his visit clothes. I block probably wouldn't be that bad.

"No lie, them niggas threw a good fifteen, bro," Sin recapped as he sat at Kelz's wooden kitchen table.

"We gonna get back. Don't even stress that," Nana said, anger pulsing through his veins. The fact that they had shot in front of his mother had him ready to kill everybody.

"So, I ain't hit boy?" Gunboy asked out loud, confused. He had seen August drop. "On God, I ain't know boy was one of them."

"Na, you ain't hit him," Beastmode clowned. "But shit was gonna happen anyway. All you hit was a bitch and a old dude. That can't be put on no scoreboard," Beastmode teased. His niece was an employee at McDonald's and had called him the second bullets stopped flying, so he had been able to investigate and put the pieces together after Sin had gotten shot at. Beastmode was a troublemaker, so the beef shit was a good time for him. Niggas tried to stay clear of him when he was on bad timing. He was big body. Six foot two inches, brolic like a football player, and known for knocking niggas out.

"At least you got what you wanted."

Money shook his head as Gunboy smirked. "You don't think, my nigga. I got a baby on the way. Niggas tryna run up a check. A nigga ain't tryna be on Rikers Island, and I damn sure ain't tryna lose my life, so I ain't playing no games with these niggas or doing dumb shit like that." He grilled Gunboy.

"We gonna figure it out," Kelz intervened. "First, we gotta figure out how to get everybody on the same page cause this shit slick divided," Kelz stated as he looked around the room. "Where Sport? Where Chedda? Where House? Niggas said everybody pull. These the main factors, and they M.I.A. How that make sense?"

"You know I don't give a fuck where House at, but Chedda o.t., and Sport went to see big bro," Money informed.

Kelz nodded. "Me and Money leading for now on," he announced. "That's how I'm putting it together for the new wave." His mind went to the conversation him and Nicole had before she left for work. "I'ma have some shit for niggas too. Give me a few days to see the vibes, but shit should be a go on the money tip." Only Money knew about the money Nicole had found, and until she was in the clear, Kelz didn't want to rely on it. But once she was, he was investing in work. A knock on the door pulled their attention. Gunboy walked to the door, looking out the peephole. His brow bent in confusion.

"You said Sport went to go see big bro?" he asked Money as he unlocked the door then pulled it open. "That's cap."

Sport walked in. "What's up?" He saluted Gunboy as they did their handshake. "Fuck everybody look like that?"

"I thought you was going to see Prince?" Kelz said as he dapped Sport.

"Yeah, I was supposed to. Shit got sticky last night," Sport said with hidden innuendo. His thoughts momentarily went to Mia. He could still taste her on his lips.

Money nodded. "Look, this beef bout to go back up and stay stuck like it was before the indictment. I'ma be honest. I'm in cause y'all my brothers, but this ain't really what I want," Money said, continuing the conversation. "All these other niggas a part of what we built and looking good off our name and sacrifices. Them the niggas that better be on front line," Money stated.

Sport looked at him like he'd lost his mind. "I hear what you saying, but everybody better be on front line. Ain't no feet up cause we already put on. It don't work like that. You should know that."

Money stood up and closed the gap between them. "Nigga, you saying that like I ain't put on. Like I ain't lose years for this shit."

Sport chuckled. "That's what come with this shit. If you ain't ready for that, fall the fuck back. Ain't no free rides cause you did shit before. This why this my shit cause I'm ready to kill or die for this shit."

"Your shit? Don't let that position go to your head. Nigga, this Prince shit. This all of our shit!"

"F.F. still on gang time. We been through too much shit to not be considered family." He looked at everybody. "So. we on some new shit. Super Loyal Family. Bro already running with that, so that's what we doing. Bro already made it known. Whoever not on that time super oppy instead. F.F. finished," Kelz stated, looking at Sport.

Flea nodded his head in agreement. Him and Prince were cousins, but he was also Prince's guidance through a lot. Flea had taught Prince a lot, and in return, Prince motivated him. He was usually quiet and let shit play out, but he felt like he had to step to the plate on this one because he could see division coming. "Niggas is family, so all the other shit, save that for them niggas. We on S.L. time." Poppy, Honcho, and Beastmode agreed with Flea. "Nana and Sin, what ya on?"

"I'm super loyal, bro," Sin stated as Nana dapped Kelz, signifying his vote.

"And who supposed to be leading the way?" Sport asked.

"Me and Kelz," Money answered.

Sport laughed. "Of course, this position went to my head, my nigga. I can't even lie," he said as he swung his hand before gripping his left wrist with his right hand.

"Copy," Gunboy spoke up as he looked at Sport funny, awaiting his answer. He slightly sat up as he watched Sport stare a hole through Kelz. It didn't matter who he was. If he moved wrong toward Kelz, Gunboy was on him. The fact that he had yet to agree was an answer in Gunboy's eyes.

Everybody looked at Sport, who turned and grilled Gunboy for a second before he scoffed then spoke. "Y'all got this new shit figured out. I got my mind set. If I ain't leading this shit, I ain't this shit," Sport told them before leaving the apartment.

"Smith, what's going on?" the CO greeted Prince as he entered the searched area just outside of the visiting room. "Go through the metal detector and clear the B.O.S.S. chair. Any jewelry? Belt?" He sat in his seat and wrote down what he had and wore. After walking through the metal detector, Prince was patted and frisked then allowed onto the visit floor. He walked up to the CO desk and was directed to his table. He took a seat at his table and gave a head nod to a few dudes he knew. His eyes gravitated toward Mia as she walked toward him with a tray of food in her hands. His eyes roamed her body from head to toe – small waist, nice bubble butt, and perky breasts. She was fly as usual, dressed in tight, light blue jeans, a white Balmain shirt, and Yeezy 350 sneakers on her feet. Her blonde hair with brown highlights was wild and curly, and her makeup was on fleek. The face mask prevented him from seeing her smile.

"Hi, handsome," she said as she sat across from him, staring at him, taking him all in and hoping he couldn't see the betrayal in her eyes because, for some reason, she felt like he would sense it.

"Wassup, Ma?" Prince pulled on the end of her hair. Mia knew he wasn't affectionate, so even the smallest gesture was appreciated. "What took you so long?" he asked, looking at the clock. She was two hours late. "And where Sport at?"

Mia could instantly feel her armpits begin to sweat. "Um, he didn't come, and traffic was crazy." She looked away nervously. Prince chuckled. He didn't know why he really expected him to pull up. "You want this right now?" she whispered, referring to the two loonies filled with drugs that she had in a chip bag and trying to divert his attention from his line of questioning.

"I'll grab it. What's up tho? Talk to me," he told her as he began eating out the bag of chips. He quickly cuffed one of the loonies in his hand.

"There was a shooting in the McDonald's on Vansiclen yesterday," she informed him as he placed his hand inside of his pants and boothed the loonie. "It was also one on Cleveland."

"Word?" Prince asked, feigning concern as he repeated the motions. Honestly, he really didn't give a fuck what happened out there. "Niggas be aight."

"Why do you fucking do that?!" Mia hissed. "You act so fucking emotionless."

Prince's face twisted in confusion. "Fuck you talking bout? Shit happen every day, so what?"

"It's more than that! I couldn't even get a hug or a fucking kiss, bro!" Mia snapped emotionally.

"Bro, you tryna argue right now. If that's what you came for, you shouldn't have came."

"If the bitch on your arm was here, you would of kissed her!" she spat.

Everything Sport told her fueled her on, and her guilt was chewing away at her. She had to turn the tables because if she didn't, there was no telling what she would do.

Prince's face grew serious. "Fuck off the floor before I make a movie."

Mia's eyes grew wide in shock. She had fucked up and pushed too hard, now he was pushing back. "You dead ass? If you make me leave, this my last…"

"I don't give a fuck what you talking bout," Prince told her.

"Over a bitch that got a whole ass baby!?" Mia replied, eyes misting. She instantly regretted it, and at that moment, she hated Sport. She hated herself, and she hated Prince. She hadn't seen any emotion in his eyes until she spilled that tea.

She had a baby… Prince thought to himself. That sadness he felt quickly turned to anger. Angel was his past, but Mia knew that neither her or any other female could compete or compare. Angel was off limits as far as conversation went, and the look in Prince's eyes said it all. They were over.

"I'm sorry…" Mia whispered.

***

Sport took a swig from his cup of D'usse before putting it down and turning to Geek, another member of Forever Famous. "We on our own time, bro. Fuck what they doing or talking about. House teaching me that unemployment shit too. So, we bout to chew." They were lounging in a hookah lounge in the hood. Bitches were all around, and the vibes were relaxing, but Sport was on ten. It had been hours since he walked out of Kelz's crib, but his anger didn't lessen a bit. His mind was made up. Anybody that wasn't with him was against him, and he wasn't sparing any opps.

Geek nodded his head as he ate one of his hot wings and listened to Sport speak. "I'm riding with you, bro. Those the guys tho, so hopefully shit smooth over. Feel me?"

"Ain't nothing to smooth over," Sport said stubbornly. Their history meant nothing to him. If niggas weren't going to follow suit, they were getting left where they stood. "Fuck them niggas," he spat as his phone vibrated. He looked at his screen and smirked. It was Mia asking where he was at. He quickly texted his location. Sport looked at Geek and thought about hiding the treason but decided against it. Geek's reaction would show where his loyalty laid. Fifteen minutes later, he watched Mia walk in then look around until she spotted him. He stood as she walked in his direction, causing Geek to look up. "You good?" Sport asked when she approached his table and gave him a tight hug. He could tell that she had been crying and figured it had something to do with Prince.

"Uh huh, you was right." Mia sniffed, embarrassed. Prince had broken her down, and she needed Sport to boost her confidence back up. Sport nodded, conscious that Geek was watching the exchange. He sat, surprised when Mia sat on his lap and took a sip from his cup. Sport could see the shock on Geek's face too. They sat silently, listening to music and eating wings, all three of their minds running wild until they heard a familiar voice.

"Facts?" Diddy scoffed as he crossed the room with Gunboy and Flea. "That's how ya doing my brother?" he asked as his eyes took in the disrespect. Mia's face had been hidden in the cuff of Sport's neck, but anybody who knew Mia could spot her from her signature hair-style. Her on Sport's lap had them all at a loss for words. Mia diverted her gaze from Diddy, Prince's seventeen-year-old brother. He was the last person she expected to see when she decided to run to Sport. Diddy had bumped into Gunboy and Flea while leaving his shorty's crib and decided to tag along. The funny thing about it was Sport's little sister was his shorty, and he was just defending Sport as Gunboy told him what had transpired at Kelz's crib. An arrogant smirk played on the corner of Sport's lips. He could feel Mia trying to raise up and remove herself from his lap, so he placed his hands on her thighs to keep her there. The cat was out of the bag, and he honestly didn't give a fuck how it made him look.

"Big facts," he revealed cockily.

"Fuck that bitch. You know bro ain't stressing her," Flea told Gunboy and Diddy before they could react. He knew that they were both young niggas who acted before they thought.

"Nigga, fuck you," Mia responded back, her cheeks hot from embarrassment and anger.

"Ho ass bitch for a ho ass nigga," Gunboy stated as Flea pulled him and Diddy away.

They took a seat a few tables away and ordered their food. Diddy's leg bounced as he kept his eyes on the back of Sport's head. He thought about the smirk Sport had on his face, and it infuriated him. He watched as Mia kissed Sport on his lips and shook his head before standing up and heading toward the bathroom. Diddy closed the door behind him and gripped the sink as he looked in the mirror. His girl would be mad, but how could he watch the fuckery and just sit there? He couldn't just not do something. Disrespecting his brother was like disrespecting him. He looked down at the bucket of construction tools that had been left in the bathroom and contemplated his next move. Diddy grabbed the tool on top, a hammer, and walked out the bathroom, bypassing the table Flea and Gunboy sat at.

"Move, bro!" Gunboy alerted Flea. Diddy neared Sport as Mia was whispering in his ear, and before Geek could look up and put Sport on point, Diddy closed in and swung with all his might, connecting the hook of the hammer with Sport's cheek.

"Arggg…" Sport screamed and pushed Mia off of him. The hook had pierced his cheek, and when Diddy pulled back, Sport's face opened so wide that you could see his tongue as blood squirted and spilled. Sport rushed Diddy, causing him to crash into a table. Flea snuck behind him, grabbing him, as Gunboy and Geek went at each other. They were separated, and employees begged them to leave as Diddy watched as Mia stood by Sport's side, crying. Now there was no doubt that their friend was their enemy.

PRINCE GRABBED HIS TABLET AND CHECKED THE TIME. HE HAD BEEN staring at the ceiling for hours with his heart heavy and mind on destruction. He had never felt as hurt as he was feeling at the moment. The thought of Angel allowing another nigga to live the dream they had dreamt of together was too much for him to digest, and for the first time in ten years, he shed tears. They hadn't spoken in over a year. The last he had seen her was when she had come to visit during a prison festival. The visit was supposed to be for closure, but they ended up fucking in a porta potty, and when she walked out, he knew it would be the last time he would ever see her. They had started off as close friends then grew a strong relationship. Somewhere along the line, it had fucked up, and he lived with the regret daily. Her having a child was a shot to his heart. Prince needed to take the pain away. Every song reminded him of her. Every TV show and commercial did too, so he sat in the dark, his anger growing by the second. Somebody had to feel what he was feeling. They said hurt people hurt people, and right now, that statement was about to take form. Nobody would feel it emotionally, but he was about to physically inflict pain. Prince dug into his pants pocket and could feel a folded paper. It had slipped his mind that it was even there. On his way back from the visit, a dude had stopped him and asked him what company he was on. After Prince told him, the dude asked him to deliver the kite to a dude named Mula who was a few cells down. Usually, Prince didn't play messenger or delivery man. You never knew what you were actually getting yourself into, and by adding yourself into the equation, you now held a form of responsibility in the situation, whether it was a drug deal or a hit. In prison, the messenger got shot too, so there was no sense in telling a nigga "don't shoot the messenger". Prince minded his business and handled his own. The only reason he had even done it was because this dude had called him by his name, although Prince didn't know him. His nerves had always been bad, and his instincts had never stirred him wrong. Something was telling Prince to read the kite. He unfolded the kite and shook his head as he began reading.

TARGET: MULA

Ayo, bro. I heard all about your situation, and once you take a deal, you good and green. Your deal on your company. His name Prince Moneyy. Long story short, boy killed a female in his case that was like family. Nuff said! Take care of that. Soon as ya pop out, I got u a hoodie.

PRINCE LAUGHED AS HE PINCHED THE BRIDGE OF HIS NOSE. THESE niggas were so bold and stupid to hand him a kite to get himself cut. He laughed harder at the one sending the message. While on Rikers Island, him and Loopy had been cool. They had been neighbors and ate together, got money together, and chopped it up daily. But when Prince was sent to the box and they separated, shit got mixed up, and Prince ended up bagging Loopy's bitch. That had been six years ago, but ever since then, anytime they were in the same prison, Loopy tried to get Prince touched. The last missile he had sent, Prince was still affiliated, so he was able to send one of his own at it. Now that he was neutral, Loopy had the upper hand, or so he thought. The funny thing was Loopy was trying to justify it by saying he knew Dream when Prince was the one who told him about the case. Loopy wasn't even from the same borough and had no connection to her at all. He just knew he couldn't admit that this was all over a bitch that chose. Prince removed a box of Tide from his property bag, retrieving the sharpened plexiglass that was stashed inside. He now had two niggas to take his anger out on. The fucked-up part was that Mula was just guilty by association.

"Walking!" somebody announced, informing inmates on the tier that a CO was strolling down. Prince quickly tucked the shank in his boxer briefs and placed the Tide box by the toilet. "Twelve cell… Smith, legal mail," the CO called out from in front of his cell. Prince pulled the sheet aside, signed his name for his legal mail, and was given an envelope addressed from the Brooklyn Supreme Court. He hurriedly removed the letter and began to read. "Motion by defendant/appellant prose to vacate conviction," he began as he scanned through the paper, his heart quickening with each word he read. "Upon the paper's filed in support of the motion and the papers filed in relation there to it is…" His eyes grew to the size of silver dollars, and his heart skipped a few beats. "Ordered that the motion be GRANTED.".

CHAPTER 4

The noise on the tier was deafening as inmates yelled back-and-forth to each other behind their gates, trying to yell over others, but Prince heard none of it. He stared at the letter, trying to register the words staring back at him. His motion had been granted. His nine to life sentence had been overturned, which meant he only had a six-year bid, which had been completed months ago. Prince shook his head in disbelief, his heart pounding uncontrollably. He felt like he was about to have an anxiety attack. He dropped the papers, placing balled fists to the wall, then rested his head on his fists. He should have been happier than ever – a part of him was – but more than anything, he was anxious and a bit terrified. For the past eleven years… six months… twenty-four days that he was gone, he had plotted some evil shit. Prince had missed a lot, and he would have to adapt to the new and unknown. He would have the opportunity to face the people who shitted on him, the people who had left his side when he needed them, and he knew how he would react. He didn't know whether he would be coming back or murdered, but it would be one or the other for sure. There would be no nine to five working or nonprofit running. He couldn't get back the time he'd lost, and he probably didn't have a lot of it left, so Prince was about to crucify motherfuckers for their sins and live every second like it was his last. He wasn't going out there to play catch up. He was taking the lead on his own terms – no regrets, no remorse, and no room for error.

Prince's gate cracked open, jarring his attention. He pulled it open and stepped out. "Kiosk!" the CO yelled down to him before disappearing. Kiosk meant you had fifteen minutes to sync your tablet, download your shit, and lock back in, so the next man could be afforded the same privilege. Prince walked down the tier, passing Mula the folded note as he did, then went to the kiosk and logged on. He had a bunch of messages, but the first one caught his attention.

"Word," he said when he read a message from Kelz informing him of everything that had gone down. He didn't think his anger could intensify, but it did. Mia and Sport? That quick? She had just left the visit hours ago. For her to have run to Sport meant it wasn't the first time. Prince was glad he had never trusted her. He was mad he ever trusted Sport. He wasn't even mad at the act. The disrespect had him furious though. Niggas would always break bonds over a bitch. His niggas were supposed to be different. But Diddy getting involved wasn't what he wanted. He began to type a reply to Kelz. He sent the message, debating whether to tell Kelz he was coming home sooner than expected, but decided to keep the news to himself for now. Prince logged off and headed back up the tier, deciding to read the rest of his messages on his tablet. He could see Mula's hands outside of his gate moving animatedly as he told a story to his neighbor. Prince spit out the scalpel from his mouth, gripping it between his thumb and index finger. Just as he neared, Prince grabbed Mula's arm, yanking him forward.

"Yo!" Mula yelled in alarm. Prince brought his own arm inside of Mula's cell and raised his arm then swiped down, once then twice, leaving three cuts from Mula's forehead to the top of his lip. Blood dripped as Prince backed away. He jogged down to his cell and locked in. He could hear Mula yelling out threats and people inquiring. He pushed all his property bags under his bed and stood by the sink, facing the gate. Once they were let out for rec, he would strike again. His panic button was too fragile to not shoot first, and if he was being honest, all the bad news he had received for the day played a big part. Even the good news was a factor.

NICOLE looked around nervously as she tapped her foot and watched cars drive by. She had received a call from the man who had left the money in the rental and agreed to meet him in order to return it. "Why the hell I ain't tell Kelz to come with me?" she said to herself as she continued to look around. She didn't even know what he looked like or what he drove. She just knew that he rented different cars weekly and had enough money to forget twenty bands under a seat.

"Nicole?" a guy who had just come off the train asked. He was short, standing about five foot six inches, and looked like he worked out. His hair was cut in a light Caesar, and beside the 18K, rose gold, men's Nautilus Patek Phillipe on his left wrist, he was plain with a white t-shirt, light blue denim jeans, and white Nikes. He definitely wasn't what she expected.

"Um, yeah, Timbo?" she asked as she went to remove the plastic bag from her purse.

"Na." Timbo stopped her. "Not right here." He laughed. "We could go into the restaurant." He nodded toward the Spanish restaurant across the street from where they stood. "I wanna thank you."

"It's nothing," she replied, hesitant about going into the restaurant with a stranger. She knew Kelz wasn't jacking no shit like that.

Timbo could sense her hesitance. "I ain't trying to bag you or nothin." He raised his hand in mock surrender and chuckled. "I just wanna thank you, show some love, and talk business."

Nicole sighed as she ran a hand through her hair. "Okay, cool."

———

THE bell rang loudly, indicating that it was time for recreation. It had been delayed because the COs had come to get Mula and escort him to medical after one walked by and saw all the blood dripping from his cuts. Luckily, he had claimed he did it to himself, so they wouldn't lock the tier down to investigate who was responsible, which Prince knew meant they were going to try to get back for what he did to Mula. Prince respected that, but it was still fuck them niggas.

Gates began opening, and his heart raced like NASCAR. He gripped the shank in his hand so tight that his knuckles turned white. His gate popped, and he could hear people mumbling. They were nervous, not knowing what to expect, and that was exactly the way he wanted them. Prince grabbed his gate, opening it, and rushed out onto the tier.

One dude tried to run toward him, and Prince swung, hitting him in his forehead with the shank. "Arg-argh," he yelled as Prince stabbed him again. The dude tried to turn and run, but Prince stabbed him again, this time in his head, causing the shank to get stuck. The dude took off, and Prince backed up, seeing who else would come his way.

When he went to turn, he felt something connect with his face, right above his eyebrow, and quickly jerked his head back before it could dig deeper. A dude had snuck up on him and cut him from behind. Spitting his scalpel out, Prince swung at the dude's facial area, swiping him on his right cheek. The dude put his head down and rushed Prince, grabbing and holding onto him. "Let go, pussy nigga," Prince said through clenched teeth as they wrestled. Prince threw an uppercut, connecting with the dude's jaw and causing him to back up. They could both hear the COs running in their direction, and the dude tried to back up and run off to get rid of his weapon. When he turned, Prince took advantage of the opportunity and grabbed him, throwing punches at his face, slicing it several times. The dude screamed as he tried to get loose. Seeing that Prince wasn't stopping, the COs began spraying them with mace. Prince released the dude and began to cough as he covered his mouth and nose. He could hear the COs giving him orders to put his hands on the gate as he looked in the direction of the other dude. Once the dude laid on the ground like the COs told him to do, Prince rushed him and kicked him in the face then was tackled and taken to the ground.

"Stop resisting," they yelled out as they punched and kicked him while one CO placed him in handcuffs. After a few seconds, they lifted him to his feet and began to pull him off the company. Prince could feel the blood dripping down his face. He couldn't believe he had been cut. As many niggas as he had cut over the years, karma had finally gotten back to him.

"So, what business do you want to talk to me about?" Nicole asked with her eyebrow raised. Timbo had given her $1,000 for returning his money and had explained a little about what he did. He was the plug. Timbo traveled once a month to Seattle to grow his own weed then got it shipped to New York. But he wasn't hands on and actually worked as a licensed discharge planning counselor on Rikers Island. He had even shown her his paystubs. Nicole could only imagine how many drugs he smuggled onto Rikers Island but was surprised when he told her that he actually didn't.

"I would never mix my illegal hustle with my career," he had explained.

Once a week, he'd received a shipment of ten pounds at different locations, rented a car, and had a worker drive to Upstate New York and Pennsylvania to get them off. He was making fifteen hundred off of each pound and feeding his niggas well, but he kept them at a distance, so robbery or greed could never be on their agenda.

"It'll help both of us if you could be like the middleman for my packages," Timbo stated.

"Woah… I'm not that type of person." Nicole grew nervous. "You don't even know me to trust me with your stuff."

"And that's why I trust you with it. You not that type of person. You just returned $20,000 to me instead of acting like you didn't find it or reporting it. This shit is simple. Since you do inventory, I could have it shipped to your job; you'll sign for it like its GPSs or some shit. Then, when my worker comes to get the rental, you give it to them, and they give you my money. It'll literally only be in your possession for a hour, once a week. Then, I'll meet you to pick up the money and pay you," Timbo explained. "I don't trust anybody, but I trust you."

Nicole's head was spinning. It was too much for her to take in at one time, and Timbo could see that she was about to decline his proposition. "I'll pay you $1,000 each package."

Now, Nicole looked at it differently. Kelz would question it. He would want to be involved, and Timbo looked like he would want discretion. She would have to balance it out because there was no way she was turning down the opportunity of a tax-free extra four stacks a month.

"When do I start?"

Sport laid in the hospital bed, dozing in and out of consciousness. The pain killers had him numb and higher than stars. His face had required stiches and had swelled to the size of a football. Mia had come in after they were done stitching him up, and Geek hadn't left his side until his girl pulled up. He was going to kill Diddy, Gunboy, and everybody associated with Super Loyal. They didn't know what they had coming, but they would regret going against him. His eyes opened when he heard someone walk into the room. It was Booga and Chucky.

"Heard what happened, Gz. We gonna get back for you. Just to show you shit real," Booga told Sport. One of his mans had been there and informed him of what had transpired, so he had decided to link Sport because, like the old saying went, an enemy of an enemy was a friend.

CHAPTER 5

Prince looked in the mirror, running a finger along the scar that ran down his left eyebrow and slightly on the side of his left eye. He was grateful that boy hadn't caught him good, and the scar wasn't as bad as he had seen or caused. An hour after the incident, after being escorted to the box, another alarm had gone off. Thirty minutes later, Prince watched as F.L. and Designer were escorted into the box as well. They didn't need an explanation. All they knew was that Prince had been cut and had stabbed somebody, so they attacked anybody associated with the ones responsible.

"Smith, you ready?" a CO appeared at his gate and asked. This was it. Prince was placed on the draft, which meant he was leaving the facility. This wouldn't be the first time. He had been transferred more times than he remembered. But this time was different because Insha'Allah, this would be the last. He was on his way to Greenhaven Correctional Facility where he would be escorted to Brooklyn Supreme Court the following day, and hopefully, he would be walking out the courtroom a free man. He placed his hands out the slot and was cuffed. They opened his cell and walked him out. Him and F.L. locked eyes as Prince passed his cell. No words needed to be spoken because what was understood didn't need to be explained. Prince had left F.L. and Designer everything that Mia had brought him, but that was just the beginning. Prince loved his niggas, and he swore that he wouldn't forget them. As long as he was able to, they would have everything they needed and wanted to be as comfortable as possible. He wouldn't do them how niggas he was loyal to did him.

He went through the process of being strip searched then was hand-cuffed and waist chained before being placed in a holding cell. He hated the process, but this time, he welcomed it. He was still shocked that this wasn't a dream. He waited as a sergeant IDed him, then he was escorted onto a bus with a few others. Due to the Covid pandemic, the usually packed bus was only occupied by seven other incarcerated individuals. Prince sat silently as the others conversed. His mind was on his plans. He had been loyal, stood solid, and gave everybody he loved everything he could give them, and in return, he had been used, forgotten, and backstabbed. He wasn't rehabilitated; he was worse actually, just more calculating, and that was dangerous. He had nothing to live for because he had lost it all – his innocence, his excitement for experiencing life, and any compassion. He had lost his bitch, his time, and every day, he was losing a little of his life. If he was released, the tables would turn. Everybody would be his pawns, and he would do something that would make people never forget who he was. Shit was about to get real. He was going to leave this world legendary and with a legacy. His name was all he had left.

Kelz watched Nicole as she waited in front of a building, texting on her phone, and wrinkles decorated his forehead. Violence was on his mind. She was his everything and looked innocent. He prayed she was because if she was doing dirt, he would kill her with his bare hands. Her hair was in a high ponytail, and she dressed in black tights that looked painted on her body and a button-down, white shirt that highlighted her B-cup breasts. Her little booty poked out, her thighs were athletic, and her stomach was flat. Her five-foot eight-inch frame didn't weigh any more than a hundred twenty pounds. Nicole had the frame of a model, and right now, Kelz wanted to lift her up and body slam her. He had intended to surprise Nicole by picking her up from work and taking her out to eat. But before he could get out and walk into her job, she had texted him, explaining that she needed to stay a little later, but to his surprise, as she texted him, she was hopping into an Uber. Instead of confronting her then and there, Kelz followed her to the building she now stood in front of.

"Yo, bro…" Sin looked over at him from the driver's side. He could see the fire in Kelz's eyes and knew if a dude approached, they would be going to jail for murder.

"Not right now, bro," Kelz replied as he pushed open the passenger side door and stepped out. Fuck waiting, he was about to break Nicole's jaw and get answers later. He took rushed steps in her direction. "You still at work?" he yelled as he approached, causing Nicole to jump, startled. Nicole felt like her heart would leap out of her chest. She didn't know what to say and knew being caught in a lie had her looking unfaithful, and if Timbo showed up at that moment, all hell would break loose.

"Baby, it's not what you think," she told Kelz, trying not to appear nervous as she pulled down her face mask. "I'm so sorry. I…"

"I'm not tryna hear shit," Kelz snapped as he slapped her phone out of her hand, causing it to smash on the ground!

Now, Nicole was scared. "Just let me explain!"

"You fucking somebody?" Kelz yelled. All he saw was red, and it took all self-control to not put his hands on her.

"No!" she yelled back. "That's what you think of me?! I know it looks crazy, but no!" Nicole could see Timbo heading in their direction with a little girl. "Listen to me please." She took a hold of his hands, but Kelz slapped her hands away. Nicole knew she didn't have much time to explain. "Baby, I swear I'm not cheating. I'm not doing anything I'm not supposed to. Well, I am but not like that. I was helping the guy who left the money in the car," she blurted out.

Kelz's anger boiled, and his face heated up. "Helping that nigga? Fuck is my wifey helping him for?!" he barked as Timbo neared. Timbo heard the comment and quickly realized what was going on. Nicole's man thought she was cheating. He tucked his daughter behind him as he peeped Sin stepping out the car. He didn't know dealing with Nicole would bring drama, but he needed her, so he had to clear the air.

"She been helping me with my shipments, my G." He held his hand out for Kelz to shake. "I'm Timbo."

Kelz looked at his hand then at his face. He frowned, stuck for a second. "Fuck you mean helping you with your shipments?" he grilled. He was ready to smash Timbo right in front of his daughter. The way Nicole stood beside Kelz let Timbo know that in order to keep his new pipeline going, he would have to add Kelz to the equation.

"Come upstairs. I'll put you on, and ya decide where we going from there. You could tell your mans to come up too."

Kelz stood for a second as he watched Timbo and his daughter go into the building. He didn't know what to think. Maybe Timbo was just covering for Nicole, or maybe they were telling the truth. He would have to give her the benefit of the doubt. "Why you ain't been tell me this shit?"

Nicole sighed. "I'm sorry. I should have, but I didn't want you to jump to conclusions. This is only the first time." She hugged him tight. "He grows his own weed then gets it shipped out here," she informed Kelz.

Kelz nodded as he called Sin over. "You could spin if you need to. Me and boy bout to chop it up."

"Everything healthy?" Sin asked, confused.

"Everything healthy," Kelz confirmed as he took Nicole's hand and walked inside. They followed Timbo up to the fourth floor and into a capacious two-bedroom apartment. They were amazed at the decor of the apartment as they stood in the living room. The cream and burgundy color scheme complemented the furniture, and the mirrored walls made it look even bigger than it was.

"This is nice," she complimented.

"It's comfortable. I'm not with being flashy. As long as my little girl got everything she want and need, I'm cool," he told them as he helped his daughter remove her bookbag. "Sky, say hi, baby." She waved at them before taking off toward her room. "I'm all she got, so it's my responsibility to give her the world. If I'm flashy, niggas gonna look at me like a robbery. A robbery could easily turn into a homicide, and I can't chance that."

Kelz understood that and respected it. "So, what's up?" he asked, getting straight to business.

"I'ma be real. I don't deal with too many people, but I could understand your position because your girl is involved. I grow bud, lots of it, and if you good at hustling and if you're interested, I could front you a few pounds at $1,500 apiece as long as you cool with Nicole continuing to do what she doing. I could start you with two."

Kelz couldn't believe his ears. This was the opportunity of a lifetime. How could he say no?

"IT DO NOT MATTER, TURN TO A SAVAGE, POCKET GOT FATTER, SHE CALL me daddy..." Lil Uzi Vert's *Money Longer* blared through the entertainment system in Sport's living room as he sat on the couch, counting up bands. *"Money got longer, speaker got louder, cars got faster..."*

He bopped his head to the music with a smirk. He had been released from the hospital and got straight to a bag. For about two weeks, House had been telling him about a new wave in the scamming loop, and seeing was believing. Due to the Covid-19 pandemic and people being forced out of work, the government was issuing people weekly unemployment income, and some were even receiving back income totaling anywhere between $5,000 and $20,000. Scammers had found a way to finesse the pandemic unemployment assistance and run up a bag. House had those shits clicking for the maximum amount, and for every person Sport brought his way, he was paying Sport $3,500, and the individual would get $4,000, while House got $5,000 and return the rest to his connect. So far, Sport had gotten three people and made an easy $10,500.

The money had kept him distracted for the last two days, but shit hadn't changed. He was going to get back by any means. The scar was a permanent one and had required close to one hundred fifty stitches to close from the inside out. Due to the force of the blow and so his stitches wouldn't rip open, his jaw was wired shut. Nana and Sin had pulled up on him at the hospital, and even Money had stopped by, but there wasn't much to speak on. The line was drawn in the sand, and he was moving forward with his decision. Kelz had been reaching out, trying to talk, but Sport blocked all lines of communication. Until they fell in line and let S.L. go, he was gunning for them and making it hard to eat like toothaches. His iPhone buzzed, informing him of an iMessage. It was Mia telling him she was coming up. She had been by his side the whole time he was at the hospital, so much so that he had to keep his girl from coming. Mia felt guilty about things, but it was bigger than her. Sport chuckled, thinking about the message Prince sent him. "We could swap out," was his only response, and Sport had to laugh at that and respect that Prince was keeping it player.

He could hear the front door open then close and looked up as Mia walked into the living room with a bag of food. Sport eyed her oiled thighs in her shorts and felt his manhood hardening. He thought back to how wet and sweet her pussy was when he had eaten it. Sport still hadn't fucked and was feigning to take Mia down. Little did he know, Mia was on a mission of her own. Prince had been on her mind, and she couldn't deny that she missed him and was regretting fucking with Sport. But she knew the damage was done. Mia didn't doubt that the news had made it back to Prince and knew for a fact that in his eyes, she no longer existed. She needed Sport to assure her that she hadn't made the wrong decision because she was a second away from driving to beg for forgiveness. She placed the bag of food from the Spanish restaurant on the coffee table next to the money and sat on Sport's lap, feeling his hardness press against her thigh. Mia pecked his lips as she rubbed the side of his swollen face.

"I got you the soup you like and applesauce," she told him. "It's healing good," she said as she looked at the scar. Guilt ate away at her and made her want to fuck him more. "I wanna fuck you," she whispered as she reached down and grabbed his erection through his basketball shorts. The feeling of his dick caused her to become moist. She removed him from his shorts and began stroking him as Sport rubbed her thigh. Mia got off his lap and down to her knees as she continued to stroke him. She leaned forward and took him in her mouth, coating it with her saliva. She gagged as Sport guided her, groaning at the pleasure she was giving him. Sport played in her curly hair as Mia's head bobbed up and down, sucking and slurping, wetting his dick up. She removed him from her mouth, stroking him as she licked the head, then placed him back in her mouth. Sport's toes curled as he watched her eat it up. The head was aight, but he wanted to be deep inside of her.

"Come here," he told her, removing his dick from her mouth and hand. Mia stood and allowed Sport to unbutton her shorts and then slide her shorts and panties down her legs. Her pussy was wet, and he could smell her arousal. He gave it a long lick before he stood up and walked her to the bedroom where he laid her on the bed then covered her body with his. He guided his erection to her pussy, and they both gasped when he pushed inside of her. Mia's pussy was tight and warm. Sport buried himself deep, causing her to moan out loud, then pulled back until only the head was drenched in her wetness. He placed his hand on her thigh, pushing it back, as he began to stroke her faster and harder, and her nails scratched his back up. He needed her to fall in love with the dick, so he began fucking her harder, beating her pussy up, and making her scream out in pleasure. His own nut was building, so he pulled out, giving himself a second before sliding back in.

Her back arched, and her pussy gripped his manhood as he pounded her, causing her to bite his neck. The feeling was amazing, and Mia moaned, enjoying every second, every inch. "Right there. Please don't stop…" she moaned. Then, she felt him cumming inside of her and was disappointed that she hadn't gotten hers too.

"Fuck," Sport groaned out as he nutted then pulled out. Mia's pussy was good and all, but it wasn't worth a swap out. All he wanted was bragging rights. He had fucked Prince's bitch. Now, she was old news, yesterday's paper.

"He was your best friend. Don't you think we're fucked up for this?" Mia asked as Sport sat next to her, wiping himself off. Now that the deed was done, she felt dirty. If she was being honest, the few minutes wasn't worth it. She hadn't even cum. Sport laughed bitterly then turned serious.

"He was before he caused a war that took time from me and got some of my closest friends killed." He spoke words he had kept in for years. "He got life in prison; he should be the last of your worries."

THE NEXT DAY, PRINCE SAT ON THE BUS, BEING ESCORTED TO Brooklyn Supreme Court, and his heartbeat increased with every minute. He was beyond anxious. He had been gone for too long and knew everything would be different and wouldn't happen exactly the way he planned. He would have to take it slow and be patient, two things he wasn't fond of. People would jump on his dick and want to be his best friend, but Allah forgave; he wouldn't. He could just imagine the look on motherfuckers' faces when they saw him free. He made a few calls the night before. He wanted to call Mia but didn't. She had every dollar to his name, and for that reason alone, she would be his first stop. The fact that she was fucking Sport didn't move him at all. Any female he checked off his checklist, he wasn't checking for. All he wanted was his money. His calls had been to Kelz and, surprisingly, Gunboy since he hadn't been able to catch Money or House. Him and Gunboy had never really built a relationship, but he had heard how youngboy was loyal and putting on, and that was the type of people he needed around him to do what he had planned. Then, there was Abby and Banko. He couldn't wait to run into them. The most dangerous thing he had learned in prison was how to control his emotions, so they wouldn't see it coming. Nobody would. Banko was first. Abby would get hers later.

The bus pulled into the basement of the courthouse, and Prince was escorted into the building and up to the second floor where the noise was deafening. "Where do you want Smith?" the escort asked the court building CO.

CO Edwards looked over his court log and scratched his head. "I actually have no room for him down here." He paused as he looked over Prince's paperwork. "His court part is upstairs anyway, take him up to the third floor," he instructed before picking up the phone.

Prince was then escorted to the elevator and upstairs where, unlike the second floor, it was quiet. "I was told to bring him up here," the escort told the female CO. CO Mejias looked up at Prince. It had been years since he had been in the court building, but she remembered him. She had been one of the COs that sympathized with him.

"Yeah, his troublemaking ass." Prince laughed as the escort officer removed his restraints. CO Mejias then walked him over to a holding pen and locked him in. Prince put his bag down and looked around. He locked eyes with the white female in the pen across from him. She had dirty blonde hair that was in a messy bun and sad, pretty, blue eyes. The beige jumper was baggy on her, and the jail slippers looked a few sizes too big. She definitely looked out of her element, but she was gorgeous.

Fuck is she doing in here? Prince wondered. "Hi."

She gave a weak smile. "I'm Cherish." She introduced herself. She stood and approached the gate.

"Prince," he replied.

Cherish nodded. The females at the jail hadn't been friendly, and she hadn't been able to reach her best friend, family, or boyfriend. So, she was craving conversation. "What you in for?" Cherish asked the first question that came to mind.

Prince laughed. "I was wondering the same shit about you."

Cherish sighed. "They charging me with looting, possession of stolen property, and grand larceny." Looting had become a big thing in the United States following the death of George Floyd, a Black man who was murdered by a racist cop in Minneapolis. The Black Lives Matter movement had called for non-violent protesting, but in some neighborhoods, it had become violent, leading to looting, attacks on cops, and even burning down businesses.

"Damn… you don't look like the type to steal," Prince commented.

"Cause I'm white?" she shot back.

"Cause you fire." Prince laughed, flirting and causing her to blush. "Where you from? What's your ethnicity?"

"You never answered my question," she replied. "But you asking a lot."

Prince laughed again. He liked her style. "I been locked up since 2009 for murder."

Cherish's eyes went wide. "You don't look like the type to kill."

"Cause I'm handsome?"

This time, it was Cherish's turn to laugh. "I'm from Germany, but I been living in the States since I was ten, sixteen years. First, Florida, then New York, Queens, and now, I live in Bushwick."

"I used to be out in Bushwick heavy. I'm from East New York though," Prince told her as he dug in his bag, removing a few snacks. "You hungry?"

"Starving!" Cherish's mouth watered at the sight of the snacks. "I been eating nothing but bullshit for three weeks!"

Prince passed her a bunch of shit. "Your boyfriend not holding you down?"

"I look like I got a boyfriend?" Cherish asked sassily.

"You look like you got a fanbase." Prince flirted back. They were equally enjoying the conversation, despite the environment.

"My so-called boyfriend hasn't checked on me one time; he even changed his number. I don't have much family here, my mom and brother, and I haven't been able to reach my best friend in days. So, no, I don't have a fanbase. I actually never felt so alone in my life." She wiped her eyes as they began to water.

Prince knew that feeling well, and for some reason, he felt for Cherish. "What they talking at court?"

"My bail is $15,000. They haven't said anything else really. They just adjourning it," she informed.

"I should be going home today. If I do, no funny shit, I'ma bail you out," he told her, not understanding why he felt the need to, but he was serious. He couldn't leave shorty on stuck.

Cherish looked at him with a raised eyebrow. "Why?" she asked. She had been through a lot – bullied, abused, used, taken advantage of, and forced to do things that she didn't want to because people thought she was too naive or because she had a big heart. Besides her homegirl, Jordyn, she couldn't remember the last person who fucked with her genuinely. Only time could tell if Prince was the second.

"Everybody needs somebody." He shrugged. "I been there – left for dead, hoping somebody would have my back just because." He paused. "Just know I got you."

"I don't believe that because you look like you got a fanbase," Cherish joked, lightening the mood. "I heard how females leave dudes in jail, but if I was your girl, I'm not leaving all that sexiness," she said, causing Prince to laugh.

"I ain't stressing no female, Ma," he told her. "I'm a real one. You look like you need a real friend."

Cherish felt like she wanted to cry. "My friend is a paralegal. I can pay you back." A thought came to Cherish. "And if you're into like a come up," she whispered, "I can help you with one."

Now Prince was even more interested. "Come up how?"

"Like a lot of money and drugs," Cherish answered, thinking about the shit she had seen while going to re-up with her man. "I can help you too."

"I'm not doing it for anything in return, but we gonna catch that come up together," he promised. "I ain't gonna lie. I'm starting over out there, so I just need somebody I could trust."

"You can trust me," she assured. "You just promised me the realest shit ever, and you don't even know me, but I'm big on being real and loyal."

Prince nodded as he heard keys approaching. "Smith, you're up," the court officer called out as he approached. He opened the cell door and handcuffed Prince before walking him out.

"Good luck," Cherish yelled out as he left. She sat on the bench in silence, not believing the conversation they'd just had. She had never had anybody who looked out just to do it. There was always an ulterior motive, and she hoped Prince was different. "Murder?" she questioned, shaking her head. He didn't look like the type, but at the same time, he gave off this aura that he wasn't playing about his.

It turned her on so much that she felt her panties become sticky. Cherish placed her hand between her thighs, applying discrete pleasure to her throbbing center, and bit back a moan. The thoughts that ran through her mind were kinky. The things she wanted to do to Prince, nasty. She pushed her hand inside her panties, and her warm juices coated her fingers as she pushed two inside herself. She winded her hips, riding her fingers and not believing her freaky ass was masturbating at court. She was so wet that her box made sound effects. Her face twisted in pleasure; she wanted to cum so bad, but the jingling of keys caused her to remove her hands, leaving her panting and frustrated. She was definitely fucking Prince after he bailed her out.

Prince was escorted into the courtroom, and his eyes went to the pew. He smirked when he spotted Kelz with a female next to him, waving at him. He approached the defense table and sat next to his attorney. "Hello, I'm Austin Davey, and this is my assistant, Silvia Beverley," the attorney introduced. "We will be representing you on your motion that was granted, and today should be your first day as a free man." Austin smiled.

Prince took everything in and was ready to move on with the procedure. "Is this time served or dismissal?" he asked.

"It's time served. If you want to…"

"I'm just trying to get home asap." Prince cut him off. Fuck a lawsuit, he'd get it in the streets.

"On the part seventy-three calendar, calendar number five, appellate division docket number 03261 of 2020, Prince Smith. Defended is incarcerated produced before the court," the court clerk spoke. "Appearances please."

"Austin Davey, attorney for Mr. Smith."

The D.A. then stood. "Jennifer Prokesh for the Brooklyn district attorney office."

"I believe that we are here to grant Mr. Smith time served today." Judge Williamson read over the documents. After that, everything was a blur. Five minutes later, Prince was escorted to the back in order to grab his belongings and change into the clothes Kelz had given his lawyer.

"How'd it go?" Cherish asked. Prince's smile was bright and contagious.

"I'm going home." He quickly grabbed a pen and paper then wrote down Kelz's number. "Call this number once you get back. My word is bond. I got you." He then removed the chain from his neck and gave it to her. "Put that on your neck. It's time to level up."

CHAPTER 6

Prince walked out of the courthouse with a smile on his face brighter than the sun that was shining down on him. He inhaled the fresh air and looked around. It was unbelievable, mind boggling, that he had made it. He thought prison was where his story would end. He thought he would never see the streets again with no handcuffs or shackles on. A lot of people thought that, but there he was. Free. Grown up. Glowed up. The sun highlighted the glow he had heard a nigga would have when he came home, and it seemed like everybody who walked by took notice. It felt good. He couldn't lie; it felt good as fuck.

He looked down at the clothes Kelz had bought him. He hadn't had time to go crazy, but the cotton, white, Comme Des Garsons shorts and t-shirt and Jordan Bred 1s were better than prison clothes. Prince removed his shirt, displaying the waistband of his Calvin Klein boxer briefs and tattooed torso.

"My fucking nigga!" Kelz embraced him. "Shit bout to get real. I love you, bro. Glad you finally home!" Prince smiled as he embraced him back. It had been a while since he had seen his boy. The female and Gunboy walked up.

"What the fuck is up, big bro? Glad to finally meet you." Gunboy dapped him then gave him a G hug.

"This Nicole, my wifey," Kelz introduced as Prince gave her a side hug. "She got us put on wit a great situation, bro. You popped out at the perfect time cause niggas bout to get rich. You know I'ma put you on your feet."

"I ain't chasing money I touched before." Prince shut Kelz's offer down. There was no way he was letting anybody lead him. He ran shit, and he was about to make that as clear as plastic. "My mindset different. I'm tryna do something epic, my nigga. I ain't really got a lot of time to do it either," he told him, causing everybody to grow confused. "I'ma show ya how to ball. If niggas ain't Super Loyal, fuck is they doing wit me?" he asked rhetorically.

"We here till the death, big bro," Gunboy vowed, growing excited. "Niggas gonna lose they minds when they see you here."

"Na, I'm lowkey wit it. I gotta pull up on Mia too," Prince told them as they walked to the grey Ford Fusion that Kelz had rented. Kelz looked at Gunboy. It was only his first hour home, and he was already on bad timing.

"Bro…" Kelz started, but Prince cut him off.

"Like I told you, I ain't stressing her and Sport. Shorty wasn't mine to begin with. She got my money though, and I need mines."

"Niggas been tryna get a line on her, but she playing the cut. We gonna get that breech, but we gonna set you out anyway, bro," Kelz told him. "We see her when we see her."

"I need a cut and shit." Prince ran his hand through his beard. "You know I'm bout to pop out. Turn a pandemic to a bandemic."

Kelz smiled hard. "You don't even know, bro."

"Big facts," Gunboy added. "It was hard times, nigga, now it's our time."

DIDDY SAT ON THE ROOF OF A PARKED CAR, SIPPING FROM A Styrofoam cup of Morir Soñando, a Spanish drink consisting of orange juice and Carnation milk, and waited for the customer to come downstairs. Two nights ago, Kelz had pulled up on him, wanting to discuss a few things. After telling Diddy to let the beef with Sport go, he had fronted Diddy two ounces he had gotten from Timbo. Timbo had told Kelz he wanted $3,000 back. So, Kelz had put his niggas, that knew how to hustle, on. Diddy, Money, Poppy, and his homegirl, Odyssey, would each get two ounces at a time at $200 an ounce, making a whole pound straight profit for him and putting them on their feet. Diddy quickly got on his grind like Tony Hawk. The pandemic had weed suppliers bougie. Everybody was pushing top shelf bud for high prices and running around with menus. An eighth was going for $100, and an ounce was going for at least $500, so the play Kelz was giving them was a great one. He just had to get a steady clientele. He watched as the door to the building opened up, and the Spanish chick who he had given his number to the day before walked out. Diddy took a second to appreciate the sway of her hips in her shorts. From what he had seen the day before, shorty had an ass like a horse. Her name was Tammy. She had recently moved on the block with her baby father and son. She looked to be about twenty-five years old, which meant she had Diddy by eight years. She stood five foot two and was a red bone with glasses. Her body was banging, and she was pretty with her brown hair and a heavy accent.

"What's up?" Tammy greeted him as she got close. Diddy openly admired her curves as she stood in front of him. His eyes went from her eyes, down her body, to her toes in her sandals. He smirked as he passed her the eighth she had requested. Tammy grabbed it from his hand and held out the $50 bill. But she held onto it when Diddy grabbed it. They locked eyes, both smirking as they held the $50. "How old are you?"

"Grown," Diddy replied. He didn't give a fuck that she lived with her man. This was the block he had been raised on. So, if he wanted it, he was going for it, and he definitely wanted Tammy.

She shook her head with a laugh. "Have a good day and put your mask on." She backed away, never breaking eye contact.

"I'm too handsome for a mask," Diddy replied, giving her a head nod. Tammy shook her head, turned, and walked inside, giving Diddy a show he could commit to memory. "I'ma snatch that," Diddy said to himself as he pushed the $50 bill into the pocket of his basketball shorts. He got off the car, and before he could walk away, the door to

Tammy's building opened, but this time, it was Pun, her man. Pun gave Diddy a head nod as he walked in his direction, unlocking the snow-white BMW Diddy had been sitting on. He climbed behind the wheel and pulled off.

"See, watching him got you off point," Kelz said from the driver's seat of his car as he pulled in.

Diddy was definitely off point. He shook his head. "My brother a boss, fuck that make me?" Diddy asked cockily. "Something happen to me, every opp shot."

"Heard you, lil nigga. I got a surprise for you though." Prince climbed out the backseat, and Diddy thought he'd seen a ghost.

"Na," he said, shaking his head. "My brother home."

"WHY DID YOU BRING HER STINK ASS OVER HERE?" LANI SHOOK HER head at the complaint. She should have known it would come, but after her long morning, she hoped it didn't. She sat on the edge of the bed and removed her Chanel sneakers.

"Bro, my feet hurt, and I got a headache. Please don't start ya shit," Lani snapped.

Abby scrunched her face up then grilled Tuti. Tuti was Lani's younger sister from her mother's side, and her and Abby couldn't stand each other. A lot of females couldn't stand Tuti actually. Like Lani, shorty was a baddie. Being that her father was from the Philippines, she had cute, Asian-like features – chinky eyes, soft lips, and a cute button nose with a high yellow skin tone. The Colombian side gave her a nice, toned, fun-sized body. She was tatted up like Lani, but she didn't carry the same class. Niggas jocked Tuti, and she ate up the attention. She was twenty-four and living her life to the fullest. She had two kids and worked as an accountant, but bitches all felt like she was just another thot that couldn't be trusted around niggas.

"Bitch, you wish I stinked," Tuti replied as she sat close to Abby purposely and stuck out her tongue. Lani blew out a forceful breath of air, exasperated.

"Ya two really got issues," she said as she removed a bank envelope from her purse. "Let me count this money so I can get away from ya." She pulled out stacks of cash and placed it on the bed. Abby watched her and felt like she couldn't breathe. Lani reminded her so much of Dream. She remembered how Dream would come home after a transaction with a bank envelope full of cash and count it while they spoke. Abby began to hyperventilate as flashbacks of the night her sister died came to mind.

"Yo, you good?" Tuti reached over and rubbed her back.

Abby jumped up and rushed out of her room and into the bathroom. She splashed water on her face as she stared at herself in the mirror. That one night had changed her life. It had killed her spirit in ways no one would understand. Banko had spared her physically, but mentally, he had murdered her in cold blood as well. For some reason, she had woken up that morning with Prince on her mind heavy. She felt like shit on a daily basis for leaving him to take the blame. But there weren't too many choices in the matter. She had taken care of him discreetly and regretted the choice of stopping. She had gotten caught sending him money one time, and the repercussions were enough to scare her straight. Abby wanted to reach out to him so bad – send him money, some pictures, something.

The knock on the door startled her, causing her to jump. "Yeah?"

"Boo, you okay?" Lani asked, concerned.

Abby wiped her face then opened the door. "I'm okay." She gave a forced smile as she walked back into her room. She sat on the bed and grabbed her phone as Lani joined Tuti with counting the money. Abby looked at the money, and it never ceased to amaze her how they were living. They were fortunate that Dream had taught her how to make a fortune. Now, Abby was always a step ahead with the loops and was responsible for a lot of scammers scamming.

Lani was the brains of the operation hands down, but everything still came across Abby's desk first. So, while everybody was doing the pandemic unemployment assistance scam, she had given her younger brother that wave while her and Lani were taking it a step further. The Coronavirus Aid, Relief, and Economic Security Act, or CARES, was a program designed to provide fast and direct economic assistance for American workers, families, small businesses, and industries. The

CARES Act implemented a variety of programs to address issues related to the onset of the COVID-19 pandemic. Abby and Lani were claiming to be sole proprietors of small businesses and stating that they employed X amount of individuals and what the gross revenue for the months prior to the pandemic were.

They were filing fraudulent EIDL loan and grant applications. EIDL was a program that provided small businesses with low interest loans. Based on false representations, the small business administration had just approved a $42,500 loan and $10,000 grant. Abby and Lani were both profiting $17,000 apiece off this one hit. She knew the least she could do was push Prince a quick band or two, especially when it was literally pennies to her.

She went to the inmate lookup website. It had been a while since she checked up on him. She paused when she heard her brother's voice. Seconds later, he walked into her room, and the sight of him made her smile. "Big head, what's poppin?"

He gave Abby a kiss on her cheek then Tuti before standing in front of Lani and looking down at her while licking his lips. Lani looked at Loso and couldn't help but giggle. He had been on her body for a long time. He was handsome and charming; she gave him that. Carlos Cooper, aka Loso, was a young nigga who was winning. Bitches loved him, and he was known to sling dick, which was why Lani stayed clear. He resembled Chris Brown with his baby face and dark Caesar but had the same hazel eyes as his sisters and a prominent dimple on his left cheek. Tattoos decorated his body, and he had plenty of drip. In a way, he was like the Prince everybody remembered.

A Cuban choker set on his neck with a bust down money bag medallion, and on his left wrist was a Rolex Sky Dweller. Loso stayed in the latest fashion like he was a rapper. All his niggas bopped a little different and liked to show out. They didn't need a team, but they were definitely well known. Him and his right-hand man were outside for real. They weren't street niggas, but they were in the streets. They both got to a bag, and everybody knew Loso wasn't to be fucked with because of Abby's fiancé.

"Lani, wassup wit your sexy ass?" Loso rubbed her chin.

"Make me fuck you up," she threatened playfully, moving her chin away. Tuti rolled her eyes.

"You need to just quit already. You're wasting your time," she stated as she began counting money, taking a glance at Loso then Abby. She had always lowkey wondered what a threesome with Loso and Abby would be like. The thought turned her on.

"He don't want none of this. Shit is addictive." Lani bit on her tongue sexily as she rubber banded a stack.

"Let me get addicted then." He shrugged as Tuti slapped the back of his head. They all laughed, and Abby shook her head at her brother.

"Leave her alone, boy. Fuck wit the stink ho," she shot at Tuti. "You know she giving it up quick and easy."

"I'ma slap this bitch, dead ass." Tuti looked over at Abby. "Ain't shit about me stink, bitch." Tuti put the money down, stuffed her hand inside her tight denims, ran a finger along her slit, then pulled her hand out. "Here, bitch, smell me." She stuffed her finger in Abby's nostrils while Abby wasn't looking. Abby jumped up as Loso laughed, bringing a balled fist to his mouth.

"Dirty ass bitch!" Abby shrieked, throwing a sneaker at Tuti.

"Didn't I tell y'all chill?" Lani said through the laughter. "Y'all need to get married for real."

Abby sat across the room on her dresser, fuming but secretly confused, the smell of Tuti in her nose. To take her mind off fucking up, or fucking her, she went back to what she was doing. She quickly typed in Prince's government name and clicked on his information when it showed up. Her eyes went wide as plates.

"This gotta be a mistake," she said out loud as she refreshed the page, only to receive the same information. "Oh, my God. Oh, my God."

"Sis, fuck is up?" Loso asked as everybody looked at her. Abby began to hyperventilate again as she began scrolling through her phone, looking for somebody's number. "Prince… Prince is home."

After getting a fresh cut and lineup, they had taken him to get an iPhone and a few outfits, then Prince had stopped by his mother's crib for a quick second before he spun off with Kelz and Gunboy to meet up with the gang. They were having a small, private get together at Kelz's crib. Prince arrived and was greeted by twenty niggas. There were a few he didn't know, a few he hadn't seen in years, and even a few females. He was enjoying the moment but knew a lot of the love was fake or fear. These were the same motherfuckers who hadn't reached out when he was behind the wall. Now everybody wanted to take a picture with him and post him on the Gram.

"Ayo, real quick." Kelz quieted the guys as they all stepped in the hallway to talk away from the females. "Bro home now, so niggas on a whole different type of time. Ain't no confusing. We built this, we held this shit down, but if it wasn't for him, this shit wouldn't be what it is, period."

"That F.F. shit ain't what we doing." Prince took over speaking. "I'm on family time, Super Loyal," he announced, making it clear as windows. "House," he addressed, "I gave you a position while I was gone because you was out here doing your thing, but now, it's over for that." He shocked everybody. Prince never forgot all the broken promises and lies House had told him while he was away. Nobody was exempt. "If you fucking with niggas, that's cool. I knew you for years, so ain't no love lost, but you ain't a part of what I'm building, nigga."

House stood silently. This was the last thing he expected. A lot of people he had brought aboard looked on, not knowing what to say or do. "Bro, this me."

"I don't give a fuck who you are," Prince said seriously. "Any nigga not on timing is out of it."

"You gotta go, bro," Kelz told him. They all watched as House took the walk of shame down the stairs with a few of his following behind him. It was time to set examples.

"You, you, you. Ya niggas all out." Prince pointed out dudes he didn't know. "No new friends. No friends period. Me and my brothers, that's that."

By the end, there were only ten standing. The plans Prince had couldn't afford any errors. He knew a team was only as strong as their weakest link, and he wasn't willing to bet his life on niggas he didn't know or trust. He looked at Bentley, who was talking to Sin and laughing without a care in the world. He had something special planned for his bitch ass. They all walked inside, rejoining the get together. Prince sat on the couch, and Odyssey took a seat on his lap. She was Beastmode's niece, and they had grown up together. Quiet as it was kept, she had fucked on all the bros. "Bro, you know you gotta let me put this WAP on you for the come home," she whispered in his ear, causing his dick to brick up.

Prince smirked. It was his first day home, and his dick was begging to get wet. He had a few bitches who he could have called that would've jumped on the opportunity to be his first, but Odyssey was far from dirt with her caramel complexion and slight gap between her front teeth. She was kind of thick and had a nice ass on her. She looked like Dream Doll in the face, so it was a good kill.

"I'm ready to slide," he replied. Odyssey stood up and went to retrieve her bag. "Bro, I'm bout to be out," he told Kelz and let Sin know. Sin had offered to let Prince stay at his crib until he was on his feet since he was never really home anyway. They had been friends since the sandbox, so it wasn't an issue. He had a lowkey one bedroom out in Bushwick on the darkside, and Prince gladly accepted the offer.

"Bro, that move a good one. Fuck wit your boy," Kelz whispered, referring to the business with Timbo. He had given Prince the rundown and had even offered to give him a pound to start off, but Prince declined. He had collected close to $5,000 from everybody, had a $2,200 check from his inmate account, and with the money Mia had, it would be able to hold him over until he made his own moves. Fuck chasing money he'd already touched before. He didn't just want money. He was chasing wealth and financial freedom. Drugs couldn't do that for him unless he was moving kilos, and that wasn't the case. "I already told you my outlook, bro. Fuck working for a nigga. We could book boy and take everything. You saying na, so I'ma respect that and not get involved," Prince replied. "Shorty I was telling you about got a come up for us. Money and drugs. I just want bread. You could take the drugs with the bros."

"So, you really gonna bail her out?" Kelz asked. He knew Prince always had a method, so he would support any move he was making.

Prince nodded. "Yup. I'ma find a bail bondsman tomorrow. I just need two people to sign off for me."

"Say no more, bro." Kelz dapped him up. "Odyssey waiting for you." Kelz laughed, nodding in her direction. "Tomorrow Money's baby shower. Don't wear yourself out, nigga." Prince looked at her in her red dress and nodded in appreciation. It was time to leave.

"I got somebody that wanna link you too," Nicole told him as she gave him a hug goodbye. Lani had called to confirm the news, and once it was confirmed, she was eager to fall through.

"I been running around all day. Whoever I ain't see wasn't that important, sis," he told her. "I'll see everybody at the baby shower."

They left, and twenty minutes later, they were entering Sin's studio apartment. "Okay," Odyssey said as they were met by a large, black painted room with a flat screen and queen-sized bed. Odyssey grabbed Prince's hand and led the way to the bathroom, closing the door behind them. "We can't use his bed, and I'm sure you wouldn't mind a real shower with a real bitch," she told him, rubbing his abs. She could feel her pussy growing wetter. It had been moist since she first hugged Prince. This was dick she had wanted for a long time, and from what she had heard, the just-came-home dick hit different. The thought of being his first had her ready to lose all inhibitions.

Prince quickly helped her out of her dress. As she pulled off the fabric, he took a second to caress and grope her flesh. He removed her bra as she pulled down his shorts and boxer briefs, a loud gasp leaving her mouth as she freed his dick. The length told her that he would hit deep, but the girth was what let Odyssey know that it would probably be the best dick she'd ever had in her life. She had always said Prince was too cocky to have whack dick; now, she was about to experience it for herself. A wet spot formed on the crotch of her red thong as Prince pulled them down her long, thick legs. Odyssey's pussy was chunky, and her arousal was loud as she stepped out of them, her hand on Prince's shoulder for balance as he took a seat on the closed toilet and took off her shoes.

As soon as they were off, Odyssey straddled him, and as Prince gripped her backside, she guided him into her love box. She was so wet that sound effects echoed as he slid inside of her. Prince gripped her ass at the feeling of her wetness, and Odyssey savored the fullness as she took him to the hilt. Prince landed a firm smack on her ass cheek as she began to ride him, bouncing on his manhood.

Prince took ahold of her titties, rolling a nipple between his fingers, causing her to throw her head back and moan out loud as she came, flooding his dick with her juices. He felt her cum and pulled her off his lap. He led her into the shower, and as he adjusted the temperature, Odyssey squatted, gripped his erection with both hands, and deep throated him, tasting herself and moaning around his dick. Prince gripped the back of her neck as her head bobbed, sucking and slurping as her hands stroked. "Damn, O," Prince groaned out as he watched her give him sloppy head. Odyssey sucked him for a few more seconds before standing up and facing the wall, placing her hands up high and arching her back, busting her pussy open. Prince stood behind her and guided his dick back inside of her. She wasn't as tight as he wanted, but Odyssey's pussy was wet and hot. Her ass clapped into his six pack as he began fucking her. Prince gripped her hips as he watched her ass wobble as he delivered long, deep strokes. Odyssey's moans bounced off the walls as she took his dick like a champ. He placed a hand to her lower back, and one reached around her body, squeezing her breast, as he fucked her harder and faster, causing Odyssey to explode again. She put one hand behind her, pressing to his abs and stopping him.

"Take it out," she moaned breathlessly. Her pussy couldn't take anymore, and Odyssey was a freak. She wanted it deep in her ass or in her mouth when he busted that nut.

Prince pulled out and watched as she grabbed his cum coated dick and squatted as he stood under the water, allowing the pressure to massage his back and neck. He watched as she spit on his manhood then licked from base to head.

"You too thick for my asshole, but we got other days for that. Welcome home, boo," she said before taking him back in her mouth and sucking hard. He was home, and like Odyssey's head game, it felt good as a motherfucker.

CHAPTER 7

Prince opened his eyes, looking around the room, and it took him a second to register where he was at. It had all felt like a dream. It was his first day waking up in the streets, and it felt weird not waking up to cell gates and a prison bell going off. He looked next to him and found Odyssey still asleep. Picking up his iPhone, he saw it was already close to noon. He hadn't slept that late in years, and it was needed. He sat up.

"Yo, O." He shook her out of her slumber. Odyssey opened her eyes and gave him a lazy smile.

"Good morning," she said in her raspy voice as she stretched, causing the sheets to fall to her waist and display her breasts, nipples erect.

"Good morning." Prince returned her smile. "I need a favor. I gotta bail somebody out and need two people with a job to sign off for the bail bondsman," he explained.

"I got you," Odyssey said with no problem. It was his second day home and he was bailing somebody out. Odyssey respected his realness, and because of that, there would never be a favor he couldn't ask. "I know I ain't do a lot while you was down, but if you ever need me, I'm not hard to find, boo. Especially if you need that dick sucked."

Prince ruffled her hair, laughing, as he stood and made his way to the bathroom to take care of his hygiene. Odyssey joined him, and while she put her head game down, he thought about his day. He needed to find a bail bondsman for Cherish, and then, there was Money's baby shower. He was sure the bros had posted pictures of him on social media, which meant the word had spread that he was home. He needed a gun as soon as possible, and he needed to get next to Mia. Nobody had mentioned Sport, Abby, or Banko the day before, but it was only a matter of time before they crossed paths. After busting a nut, he hopped out the shower, and after brushing his teeth, he walked out, allowing her to finish. He put on a pair of boxer briefs then dressed in light blue Mike Amiri jeans, a white Balenciaga t-shirt, and a pair of white Balenciaga runners, glad that Sin had gotten him a few things and dropped them off. He grabbed his phone and sent Kelz a text to come pick him up.

"What's up with your homegirl?" he asked Odyssey as she stepped out the bathroom in her panties and bra.

"Oh, my God." She shook her head. She had been the one to link Prince and Mia and wasn't really trying to get in the middle of their mess since she was cool with both of them. "She did bad; you fucked me. Ya even." She shrugged.

Prince had to laugh at that. "I don't care about all that. Shorty got my bread, seven bands." Odyssey's eyebrows rose. She knew how Prince had been before prison time and remembered the news vividly, so she prayed Mia didn't try to do any dumb shit with the man's money.

"I'ma hit her up," she said as she went into her bag to retrieve her phone. She had several missed calls and unread notifications. Ironically, most were from Mia. "She knows you home cause she been blowing up my phone since yesterday," Odyssey told him as she texted Mia back.

"Let her know get mines to me respectfully or I'ma get disrespectful," he stated. "I always told motherfuckers that I was gonna see them walls. Guess they didn't think it was true."

"Well, you home now so stay home, nigga," Odyssey said as she looked up from her phone. "The real ones missed you, and the fake gonna wish they were real."

Sport couldn't believe Prince was home. He had seen the pictures then got a call from House telling him about what had went down. He was stuck on stupid. Fear wasn't an emotion he possessed, but although he was a killer, Prince was evil personified. He would pull up on him when the time was right, if anything, just to check energy. Mia had been blowing his phone up all day and night, but he ignored her. He had gotten her pussy a few times and found her to be useless. She was mistaken if she thought he was cuffing her. Him and his wifey, Keya, had been together for a while, and there was no way he was swapping a dime for a penny. Mia proved her worth when she allowed him to explore her body while she was with Prince.

"I gotta figure something out," Sport said as he pressed on Nana's name. He wasn't letting what Diddy did go, and he knew Prince wouldn't let it rock after he did what he did. So, he had to be war ready. "Yo, gang, link me."

Hours later, Prince jumped out the passenger seat of Kelz's rental and walked toward the entrance of the party hall that Money and his baby moms, Tiffany, had rented. He had been running around all day and just wanted to kick his feet up and vibe. He had found a bail bondsman who accepted ten percent. After getting Odyssey and Nicole's signature and paying $1,500, he was told that Cherish would be out by midnight. They had spoken the night before, and he could hear the eagerness in her voice. She still hadn't gotten in contact with any of her peoples, and that only made Prince more determined to do right by her.

He walked into the hall with the gang trailing behind him, eight deep, and he could feel eyes on him. The black face mask kept him from being recognized, but he felt like some knew who he was. He had cockiness in his stride as he met Money at the back of the hall in front of the chair meant for Tiffany and the table decorated with balloons, gifts, and cupcakes.

Prince took in his surroundings, his eyes looking from table to table, face to face, until his eyes locked on the sexy, light skinned girl dressed in blue ripped jeans, a dressy Louis Vuitton halter top, and a pair of Louis Vuitton Archlight sneakers. Her hair was neatly pulled back into two buns with her baby hairs resting on her edges. She twerked like a professional as she bit her tongue cockily and held a hand up as the Migos featuring Cardi B and Nicki Minaj hit song, *Motorsport*, blared through the speakers.

Money smiled wide as he hugged Prince. He was at a loss for words, excited, and nervous that Prince was standing before him before expected. "My boy, I can't believe this shit. This shit made this day more special. Real shit," he stated. Prince nodded, still looking around.

"Congratulations," Prince told him. "I ain't grab no gift, but I got your little one forever."

"You the gift, bro. I owe you everything, and there's nobody I'll trust to be the godfather but you," Money told him as he waved Tiffany over. Tiffany stood, conversing with Keya, and her pregnant belly looked like it was ready to burst out of her white Prada dress. The twenty-two-inch weave in her hair dropped down to her lower back, and her makeup was done to perfection. Tiffany's skin was the color of an iced latte, and she had a nice body.

"Who is that?" Keya asked as they sauntered toward Prince and Money.

Tiffany squinted her eyes as she tried to recognize him. "I don't know," she told her as they approached. "What's up?" Tiffany asked as she walked into Money's arms. She smiled up at him, looking handsome in his Versace Medusa shirt and belt, black jeans, and Versace Chain Reaction sneakers.

"This is Prince, babe. Bro, this is Tiff," Money introduced, shocking Tiffany and Keya.

Tiffany glared at Prince, her face displaying an attitude, but Prince didn't notice.

His sight left Keya, who had captured it, and was now on the female who sat in front of the twerker. He could feel rage traveling through him. He had felt like all eyes were on him when he walked in, now he was certain that at least one pair was, and as he stared back, his face was unreadable. Looking at Abby brought murderous thoughts to his mind. He excused himself from Money and began walking in her direction as she watched him. He could smell her fear from across the room and wondered what the first thing she said out of her mouth would be. He sat at her table, directly across from her, gaining the attention of the girl who was just twerking.

"You not gonna speak?" he asked Abby. He had to admit that Abby had grown to something sexy. Abby was thick in all the right places and had long, black hair that was styled in braids. She wore Cartier glasses on her face and even smelled expensive. He could tell that she was up. Lani stood at the end of the table between Prince and Abby. They knew he would show up and still couldn't believe that he was in front of them, and like Abby, she was at a loss for words.

"Hi, Prince," Abby spoke shyly. Her heart felt like it was running a marathon in her chest. She quickly reached inside of her purse and pulled out the money she had for him. She placed the envelope on the table. "I got some bread for you, bro. I know we got a lot to talk about, but here ain't the best place." She slid him the $10,000 while looking around.

Prince looked at the money and laughed. "I see you glowed up, but that shit don't work wit me. What's up wit boy?" he asked her, referring to Banko. "You don't owe me shit, and I don't want shit from you, shorty. Boy owe me everything though, and I want mines in blood."

Abby began to sweat as she looked at Lani nervously. Prince didn't know that her and Banko were still together and engaged. If he did, he would have probably killed her on the spot.

"Hi to you too," Lani intervened, seeing the predicament her friend was in. She was the only one besides them that knew the truth but was confused about what Prince was talking about.

Prince instantly remembered her voice. "The bad." He nodded, taking his eyes off Abby and letting them roam to Lani's body. "Over here throwing that shit and all."

Lani laughed. "Welcome home, Pa," she said as she leaned over the table and pecked him on the cheek. Her aroma tickled his nose, and he licked his lips in yearning. He turned back to Abby, who was confused by their encounter.

"I might not be here for too long." He tapped the table and stood up. "You did bad, Abby. You gotta make that shit right," he called out as he walked away to join Money and Kelz. He had to put distance between them before he acted off emotion.

"She looked just like Dream, right?" Money asked as Prince sat next to him. He had been holding his breath, expecting Abby or Prince to fuck up the party. Prince nodded in response as he kept an eye on Abby and Lani.

"Banko smart. He kept that under the wing all these years, bro."

Prince looked at Money, stunned. He had to be hearing him wrong. "She still fuck wit Banko?"

"Hell yeah. They engaged and all that," Money replied.

"Yo, bro..." Kelz got Prince's attention before he could make his way back over to her. "Look."

Prince looked up and shook his head at Mia heading in his direction. She walked with purpose, and he had no time for it. He leaned over to Money. "Don't ask me why or say shit, bro. I need a gun right now."

"I GOTTA PEE. OR SHIT. OR SOMETHING. I JUST GOTS TO GO," ABBY told Lani as she bounced her leg nervously. The look in Prince's eyes was the same look he had the day Dream died, and that scared Abby to the core. She didn't fear much because she knew Banko wouldn't let anything happen to her, but Prince was somebody he couldn't save her – or himself – from. She knew how it would look from the outside looking in. Her staying with Banko should have been a no-no. He had killed her sister. But it was like her brain wouldn't accept that. Banko had come along two days after the murder, begging for forgiveness, justifying the homicide, and reminding her that she could have been dead too. He had spared her, and that had to count for something, he explained. Back then, Abby wasn't in the right state of mind. Suicide had been contemplated because the guilt was too strong. But Banko had made it all better. He was there when nobody else was and pushed her to get her shit together. Until she did.

The first time he had hit her was when he had found a letter in her purse addressed to Prince. It had been after the home invasion that she was a victim of. After her return, Banko had treated her delicately. But seeing Prince's government on an envelope had flipped a switch inside him. Banko had beat her so bad that he knocked out two teeth and broke her left arm. She should have left then, but it was like he had a hold on her she couldn't get out of. He had manipulated her to do things that broke her and made her fear him more, so leaving had never been an option. She belonged to him, and there wasn't anything she could do about it.

Years of being controlled had taken a toll on her self value and demolished her confidence. Even talking to Prince took a lot of courage. Banko owned her. Several incidents helped her to love him with those terms. Banko must have not gotten the memo that he was home because if he did, there was no way he would have let her out of his sight. Now, she feared what he would do if he found out that they were in the same place.

Nowadays, Banko was him. Thanks to Abby, his bag was way past up, and he was feared and looked up to like he was Allah himself. *This nigga is the devil though.* Abby thought about Prince and things she knew about him. "I have to leave," Abby murmured, fear racing through her veins like good dope.

"We just got here," Lani argued as she looked across the room at Prince. It was like she was drawn to him. The sight of Mia making her way over was enough to piss Lani the fuck off. It also looked like Prince was about to leave. "Nothing is going to happen to you."

"I'm talking about him." Abby slapped the table on the verge of tears. "I did bad, sis. I did so bad." Seeing Prince brought clarity. She had been living a lie and had to right her wrongs. Lani grabbed her hand supportively, realizing what she was saying and how serious she was. She had always given it to Abby straight no chaser and told her to leave Banko. The love couldn't cover the abuse. *But why now?* Lani wondered, feeling like the truth wasn't fully it anymore. She couldn't tell her that she understood because it wasn't her shoes to fit, but Lani supported any decision she made.

"Sis... You could leave. I can help you, and from everything you told me, he can help you too," she whispered the last part.

"He will kill me if I tell him I been fucking Banko since that day." Abby wiped a tear.

"Huh? Why? What are you not telling me?" Lani stared at Abby, wanting answers.

"I'ma tell you everything. But right now, I have to pee bad, and I need to leave here. I need air." She fanned herself.

Lani had her back through thick and thin, but she wasn't leaving without speaking to Prince first. She felt like she was the only one who could speak to him on Abby's behalf. Plus, the way he had turned down ten bands told her he was still bossed up and worth the risk. "Tuti is home. Go to her crib," Lani told her since Tuti lived two blocks away.

Abby scrunched her nose up like she smelled something stank. "Of course, I gotta go to the ho to save a bitch," she stated, causing Lani to laugh as she stood. "I know why you wanna stay too, bitch. You ain't slick," she leaned over and whispered in Lani's ear before playfully biting it. "Guess we both keeping secrets cause ya spoke before." She looked at Lani accusingly. Lani smirked arrogantly as Abby turned and left, heading out the party hall in a hurry. As soon as she did, Lani stood and sashayed her pretty ass directly in front of Prince before he could walk out. She could hear Mia begging, threatening to make a scene, and she had to bite her tongue to stop from laughing as she grabbed Prince's hand and tucked herself under his right arm, daring Mia to say something.

———

Abby sighed in frustration as she made her way upstairs to Tuti's apartment and knocked on the door. A few seconds later, she could hear bolts being unlocked, then the door was pulled open. "What you want, bitch?" Tuti looked her up and down. Abby sucked her teeth and pushed past her before scurrying inside the bathroom.

After she was done, she walked out and into Tuti's bedroom where Tuti sat on the bed, scrolling through social media.

"Why you ain't go to the baby shower?" Abby asked, sitting next to her and unlocking her phone. Banko had texted her several times, but she had been too busy thinking to reply.

Tuti sat up. "For what? That's ya peoples, not mines. Plus, I ain't have no babysitter, so I figured I'd just stay here and play in my pink ass pussy."

Abby whipped her head in Tuti's direction. "You need help, seriously."

Tuti grinned as she got up and stood in front of Abby. "How I smell?"

Abby leaned back. "I'm telling you now, play wit..." A lump formed in her throat when Tuti brazenly put her hand inside her panties, rubbed her pussy, then pulled her fingers out.

"How I smell, bitch?" she repeated as she rubbed her fingers under Abby's nose and along her lips. "How I taste?" she asked when Abby licked her lips. Abby swallowed as she willed herself to get up and leave, but it was like her ass was glued to the bed. Tuti's confidence was something Abby used to have, and despite how much shit she talked, it turned her on.

"Tuti, move," Abby said, her eyes closed tight. She felt Tuti's lips press against hers and couldn't stop herself from kissing her back. The kiss was full of hunger, and before she knew it, she was down to her bra and panties and sitting in the middle of Tuti's bed. Tuti kissed Abby slowly, sensually, then sucked on her bottom lip as she moved her hair out of her face.

"You still think I stink?"

Abby shook her head. "No," she whispered. In no way was she lesbian, or even bi-curious, but she'd never been handled so delicately. She had been used and mishandled, so this pleasure felt like a gift from God. Tuti unhooked Abby's bra as she planted kisses along her collarbone then took a nipple in her mouth, sucking slowly, causing Abby to moan out loud.

"Look how wet you are," she hissed as she rubbed the crotch of Abby's panties. She pulled them off as Abby lifted herself to assist. "Damn..." Tuti licked her lips as Abby's waxed pussy came into view. It was knowing that she couldn't be resisted that turned Tuti on and had her pussy leaking like a faucet. Abby had always acted like Tuti was trash, like she looked down on her. Now, she was on the verge of cumming as Tuti moved her fingers in and out of her love box. Abby felt like her body was on fire, and she would explode at any second. She raised her head and kissed Tuti, their tongues doing a sexy wine as her juices poured out of her and onto Tuti's hand. She felt Tuti plunge in knuckle deep and felt her pussy climax. Tuti kissed down her body until she was face to face with Abby's vagina and began eating her out. After a while, she climbed over Abby until they were in a sixty-nine position and went back to devouring her as Abby mimicked her every move.

———

"I BEEN CALLING FOR A FUCKING HOUR, AND SHE AIN'T ANSWERING me!" Banko barked as he sat on the couch in his and Abby's living room, a PS4 remote in his hand as he again reached Abby's voicemail. With every call she missed, he planned something worse to do to her ass. Banko wasn't used to her ignoring his calls or not following his orders. Abby was real submissive in their relationship and had been that way since the day she had accepted him back into her life. At first, he had kept Abby to ensure his freedom, but over the years, he had become confident that she wouldn't tell anybody the truth and just couldn't seem to leave her alone. The night he had killed Dream, he just couldn't bring himself to kill Abby too, and he was glad he didn't. Abby had leveled him up and helped him secure a bag he couldn't imagine getting to without her. She was the perfect investment. At twenty-nine years old, Banko had two cars, a house, and more money in the bank than most niggas in the hood. There was no way he was letting Abby go or letting her leave him. "This bitch know fucking better!" he vented to Booga.

Booga shook his head as he made Jimmy Butler score a jump shot. He had heard his fair share of Abby and Banko fights and opted to just stay silent. Last thing he wanted to do was add fuel to the fire when Banko was on bad timing. They were cousins, but he didn't respect the woman beating, especially since Abby was the cash cow that had them chewing. Banko tried her again, and she finally answered.

"Hello?"

"Hello? Bitch, where the fuck you at? You don't see me calling your fucking phone?!" he barked into the phone as someone began knocking on the front door.

"I'm bout to come home in a little. I was..." Abby stated but was cut off by his screams and threats.

After having sex with Tuti, she had rushed out and decided to take a walk. Her mind was all over the place, and she just couldn't go home yet. There would be consequences, but she was willing to accept them because they were damn sure going to be the last ones she ever received.

Loso walked into the living room and shook his head, knowing it was his sister that Banko was screaming at on the phone. They argued, fought, then were back together, so like everybody else, he stayed out of it. As long as Banko didn't put his hands on Abby in front of him, then there was no smoke. He had come over to holla at Banko about Prince. Loso had sworn he would kill him if he ever made it home.

"You gonna make me kill your stupid ass! Come the fuck home right now!" Banko barked as he stood up.

"I'll be home in a few!" Abby shot back. Abby fighting back only made him madder.

"Na, bitch, you coming home right..." He looked at the phone to see that she had hung up then threw the remote against the wall, breaking it. "I be back," he told Booga and Loso before storming out.

Prince sat across from Lani, listening attentively as she spoke. She had practically kicked Mia out and locked Prince down. They had unfinished business, she told him, and he was cool with finding out what it was. He stared at Lani and had to admit she was a baddie. He was attracted to her poise and natural beauty. Shorty was a whole vibe and had him laughing the whole time.

"I'm serious though. Don't come out here getting caught up wit these whack bitches. If you gonna let a bitch stress you out, let it be a baddie," Lani joked.

Prince laughed at that. "Na, no stress, Ma. I'm on my own time. Money, bitches, and fame. That's plan A for me."

"What if you fall in love and get a bitch pregnant?" she asked as she rested her face on the bridge her hands created.

"That's what they got Plan B for," Prince cracked, referring to the morning after pill. Lani laughed and shook her head.

"You're really a dick head," she said, causing him to join in on the laughter. The longer they spoke, the more time she wanted with him. She wasn't letting him out of her grasp. She wanted to wet his beard with the wetness that she felt between her thighs. Their vibes were magnetic, and they were in their own little world until Prince looked at the time on his iPhone. He had forgotten that he had to meet up with Cherish at her crib, and although he was enjoying Lani's company, he didn't want to keep her waiting. He sent a text to Kelz.

"I got something I gotta take care of."

"I'm not used to getting curved," Lani told him.

"You a big girl; you gonna be aight," he replied, giving her a wink then a kiss on the cheek before walking off and leaving Lani pouting.

He walked outside with Kelz and Money. "I gotta meet Cherish," he told Kelz as they stood by the rental. Money looked around before lowkey passing him the gun he had requested.

"Oh, shit, look at bro," Money announced.

Prince turned and was shocked to see Kasper walking their way. It had been five years since Prince had spoken to Kasper, eleven and change since he had seen him, but none of that mattered when they embraced. Kasper was his righthand man, and Prince had heard throughout the years that he had been down bad. So, he didn't blame Kasper; he blamed it on circumstances.

"My brother." Kasper patted his back. "It's good to see you. It's been a long time." Prince bit the inside of his inner jaw to keep his composure. Kasper wasn't the same, and it was evident that bro had been through it while Prince was gone. "I missed you, my nigga."

"We got a lot of catching up to do. I wanna fuck you up though, bro. For real!" Prince told him as they took a few steps to talk alone.

Kasper nodded in understanding. "I'm a big body now, bro." He flexed his muscles jokingly.

"I don't know…" Prince chuckled. "I don't know if I got a lot of time," he told Kasper. "I'm going to kill shit, no lie."

Kasper's face and heart dropped. "What? Na, bro." He was the only person Prince trusted with information so vulnerable.

"Ain't no tears or emotions wit it, bro. I'm home. I made it, and we about to go crazy. For real. Shit don't stop nothing. I still want all the smoke."

Kasper sniffed back his emotions, knowing how Prince was, and nodded. "I didn't expect nothing else, and you taking us to the top won't surprise me, bro," Kasper said honestly. "You ain't no regular nigga, my brother. You always been the one I expect the unexpected from. The one I know gonna make sure everything is beneficial for us. You not being here, that shit fucked me up mentally. I was down, bro. I tried to get help from the bros, family, but everybody just left me on stuck. Blocked me. Ignored me. Shit was hard, and I couldn't face you like that."

"I won't ask about the rumors cause they don't matter to me. You my brother through the worst." Prince showed Kasper the tattoo of his name in a scroll on Prince's left forearm. "Fuck everything that happened. We bout to be at our best, bro."

Kasper believed him, and for the next thirty minutes, they caught up. "You was on your way out?"

Prince looked at the time. He was sure Cherish was home by now and wanted to link her to get situated. She had invited him to occupy the spare room in her crib, and as much as he didn't mind staying with Sin, a bedroom was better than a living room any day.

"Yeah, bout to meet somebody. Come wit me, bro."

"I'm actually staying with my mom, bro. She ain't doing too well," Kasper informed. "But tomorrow, we gonna link early, bro."

They watched as Bentley got out the car, a smile on his face. "Sup, gang?" He dapped Prince. Prince returned the smile.

"Meet me up the block. I'ma walk Kasper," he told Bentley, who quickly hopped back behind the wheel as Prince and Kasper walked up the block, finishing their conversation and exchanging numbers. "Call me once you get back in the crib." Kasper gave him a brotherly hug. "You ain't regular, bro. It's your time to win."

"Our time, bro," Prince corrected as he backpedaled then got in Bentley's passenger seat.

Bentley chatted as Prince looked out the window, taking everything in. With every block they passed, he noticed that the hood hadn't changed much, just the people and their morals. As he rode, something caught Prince's eye. He quickly demanded Bentley stop the car. There, in front of the Chinese restaurant, on her phone, was Abby. Without thinking it through, Prince removed the 9mm from his waist, pushed open the door, and climbed out before Bentley could try to stop him. Prince walked around the car and in Abby's direction. Abby never saw it coming as Prince crept between two parked cars, raised his gun, and squeezed the trigger.

BOOM!

The bullet found its home in Abby's face, instantly dropping her to the ground. Running up on her, he pumped three more into her face – *BOOM! BOOM! BOOM!* –before he jogged back to the car and hopped in the backseat.

"Nigga, drive," he instructed Bentley, who was frozen in fear. Prince hit the back of the headrest. "Drive!"

Bentley pulled off, leaving small clouds of smoke under his back tires and the screeching of tires echoing through the air. He was on the verge of panicking as tears sailed down his face. It seemed like everything happened in slow-motion, and his stomach turned, threatening to erupt all over his car.

"Drive through Sunnyside," Prince instructed. Sunnyside was a dark, dead-end strip in east New York. It led to the side entrance of Highland Park and was a good spot to get low. Bentley drove onto Sunnyside then pulled over and killed the engine.

"Bro bro, what the fuck?" he stammered in disbelief as they sat in the car.

"Why you ain't tell me you was fucking with Banko?" Prince asked as he pointed the gun at Bentley.

BOOM! BOOM!

Bentley's body slumped forward as the bullets ripped through his face, killing him instantly. Prince used his shirt to wipe the door handle of his prints and then pushed the door open. He tucked the gun as he hurried through the dark park and up the back stairs that led to Highland Boulevard. He walked calmly, head on a swivel as he made his way along the boulevard enroute to Bushwick. He passed the Jackie Robinson Expressway and put a pep in his step. He knew he was bugging, but the adrenaline felt good. He had only been home two days and just finished killing two people he swore he would kill. The kills made him feel powerful, like he had just achieved a long-term goal. But it made him hungry for more – for Banko.

"Divine timing, my love." A familiar voice startled him, catching his attention. He looked at the car that was waiting for him to walk past the gas station entrance, so it could enter.

"Na, you a creep," he joked as he stood in front of Lani's car, eyes squinting to look past the bright headlights. She feigned insulted as she slightly lifted her foot from the brake, causing the car to jump forward and making Prince laugh. "You're too pretty to be scary," he said, causing her to blush, and approached her passenger seat then got in.

"And you're the cutest nigga I ever seen in my life, but I'm scared of how I feel in your presence already," she admitted.

"You ain't been in my presence long enough," he said as she drove up to a pump and passed a guy a $20 bill. She turned and faced him.

"I felt like this for a long time."

"You knew where I was at. You could of reached out," he shot back. He knew how females switched up when a nigga came home.

"My friend asked me not to. It was a mixxy situation," she replied.

The mention of Abby made him realize how dangerously he was playing. But him being in her presence right now made her the perfect alibi witness. "So, you chose your friend over your feelings?" Lani's eyebrows creased, making her appear prettier. He was definitely attracted to her attractive ass. "Love or loyalty? he asked.

"I'ma have to choose loyalty."

Prince nodded in agreement. "That just made me like you a little more," he said, causing her to laugh.

Lani drove off. "You got someone – I mean, something – to do for the night?" She tried to be funny. Prince playfully popped her chin, causing her to giggle. She didn't know how he had ended up in her presence, but she was glad that he did.

"You letting me do you? If not, na, I'm free."

Lani smirked. "Real cute. This ain't regular."

"I wouldn't be in your presence if I thought it was," he said as they sat at a red light, eyes locked. "You seem like you a different vibe. Now what?" he asked as he got lost in Lani's gray eyes. He didn't regret killing Abby. She deserved it, and he would sleep as peacefully as the night before. But he didn't want to witness how it would devastate Lani.

"Have faith in a light skin." She smiled at him. "You used to motivate me, and I'm in need of some motivation."

CHAPTER 8

Prince looked down at the burning candles and swiped a hand down his face, overwhelmed. He had to bite into his bottom lip to stop himself from breaking down, conscious of the eyes that watched his every move. Plenty of people attended the three-person memorial that was being held on his block. He could hear the voices around him. The sniffing. The cries. But he couldn't tear his eyes from the burning candle by his foot.

Prince had made it to Cherish's apartment the night before, only to find her outside on the porch with a look of defeat on her face. The lock to her apartment had been changed, and from what she could see through the window, the place was vacant. So, Prince had taken her back to Sin's apartment and allowed her to take a shower and get some rest.

They both had been sleeping peacefully, sharing the bed, when the ringing of Prince's phone had woken them up. He thought it would be somebody informing him of Abby's or Bentley's murder. He was prepared to feign shock. But when Diddy informed him that Kasper had passed away the night before in his sleep, there was no faking the tears that began to spill. They said death came in threes. Prince sniffed, trying to compose himself before the floodgates opened. He looked at the flowers. At all the people that were there showing fake ass love.

These were the same people that had turned their backs on Kasper when he was down. Blocked and ignored him. Prince shook his head then kicked the candle by his foot, sending it flying across the street and causing people to gasp in shock.

"I got you, bro. Walk wit me. I got you," Cherish said softly as she placed a hand on his bicep. Her own eyes filled with tears as she watched Prince kick another candle before she pulled him away. She felt out of place, but she was there for him. They had spent most of the night talking, and something about their connection had her stuck on him. She didn't know many dudes who would bail out a female he didn't know then give her a place to stay and not try to fuck. Prince was a real one; she was betting her last dollar on that. Prince sat on the stoop of the building they had grown up in and sighed deeply.

"Go to the crib. I'ma pay for you a Uber," Prince told Cherish. He was expecting Banko to show his face for Abby and wanted Cherish off the block. He had gotten rid of the gun, but the way he was feeling, he could kill Banko with his bare hands. Cherish wanted to protest. She wanted to show him that she was by his side, but she knew that he needed his space, plus she had to try to reach out to her best friend, Jordyn.

"I'ma go to my homegirl crib and see why I haven't been able to contact her," she informed him, resting her head on his shoulder. Prince dug into his pocket and peeled off two blue faces and passed them to Cherish.

"I'ma have somebody drive you then," he told her before calling Sin over. Since Sin was on his way off the block, he didn't mind giving Cherish a ride.

"Ayo, you know her little brother on his way," Sin whispered in his ear, putting him on point. "Loso in the field, and you know the whole Dream situation…"

Prince shrugged. "He could feel how he want. I ain't ducking no smoke, bro. Which is why I want her off the block."

Sin nodded then guided Cherish to his parked car. They pulled off, and Prince looked to his right in time to see Lani heading his way. Even in gray joggers and a tank top, her eyes puffy from crying and her hair in a ponytail, Lani was the baddest thing on the block. She invaded his space unapologetically, and Prince placed his hands on her hips as she stood between his legs, caressing his waves as she hugged him.

"Come with me," she told him, pulling back, her eyes piercing his. He allowed her to pull him up and lead him to her Benz. Prince's eyebrows rose as she unlocked the doors and lowered into the driver's seat. He got in and sat back as she started the car and drove off. They rode in a comfortable silence for about an hour, both in their own worlds mentally, trying to hold back emotionally.

Like him, Lani wasn't one to let anybody see her vulnerable. She had done a good job on holding back her tears during the memorial, but when she saw Prince on the verge of breaking, it nearly broke her. For some reason, she needed his comfort and wanted to be his. He had her at hello, and he had been on her mind since the day they spoke on Money's phone. Being in his presence made her feel like she belonged there, like if she wasn't careful, he would control every beat of her heart like a conductor. The way butterflies two stepped in her stomach told her she had fallen in love at first sight, something she had never been. The thought caused her to grip the steering wheel tightly, catching Prince's attention.

"I didn't do it," he told her, breaking the silence as he looked out the window.

"I know you didn't do it. You was with me. I knew where she was, and I think I know who did it," Lani responded as she maneuvered through traffic. Lani didn't suspect him of Abby's murder.

Prince turned to face her. "I'm talking about Dream." For some reason, he just wanted her to know. Nobody's opinion had ever mattered, but Lani's did.

"I already know that," Lani told him. "Abby told me the truth a long time ago. She always wanted to help you, but his insecure ass stopped her," Lani said as she pulled into the parking spot. Lani turned the car off and sat back. "She was my best friend. She told me everything. Banko killed Abby," she said as tears fell from her pretty eyes.

"Where we at?" Prince asked, changing the subject. He had read the sign that said New Jersey. He just didn't know where exactly they were or why.

Lani sniffed her emotions away as she unlocked the doors. "My home," she said as she stepped out.

Prince followed her inside an elevator and up to the seventh floor. There were only two doors when they got off, and Lani unlocked the door on the left before pushing it open. The first thing Prince noticed was how spacious her condo was. Three apartments could easily fit inside, but Lani didn't have it all cluttered. She could have been an interior decorator with the way she had put her sanctuary together, and Prince marveled at the details. Her wooden floors were so shiny and looked like you could eat off of them. The living room area was at a lower level, stairs leading to a circular gray suede couch sitting in front of a seventy-two-inch flat screen and entertainment system. To the left of the TV was a glass door leading to a balcony, and to the right was a dining room with a glass table and six chairs. Her kitchen area was small but comfy, separated from the open space by a bar-like kitchen counter. Two doors were straight ahead, and to the right of the entrance was another door.

Lani closed the door behind him then led the way through the door to the right and up the stairs. It led to her bedroom. A king sized, platform bed with an enormous headboard set in the middle of the grey Fendi carpeted room. There were three doors around the room and a floor to ceiling window with a La-Z-Boy recliner in front of it.

"You could take your sneakers off and sit in the bed," she called out as she kicked her 350s off then made her way into one of the doors – a walk-in closet, Prince assumed.

He removed his Yeezy 500s then walked over to the recliner and took a seat. The view was amazing, and he understood why she had placed a chair in that very spot. It was like he could see the entire New Jersey. But the sight of an armored truck held his attention. He wondered if money could take all the pain away because it seemed like nothing else could – not even being free. Kasper wasn't supposed to die. It just made no sense, and Prince felt at fault. He had gone into cardiac arrest while sleeping, and Prince felt like if he would have called him like he was supposed to, maybe he would have woken him up. Or maybe Kasper dying was karma for the murders he had committed. It was like it was meant for them to have that talk. Their last conversation would be their last conversation ever.

The sound of Lani returning broke him out of his thoughts. She approached him with stacks of money in her hands and took a seat in his lap, facing him. She looked at him with teary eyes. "Being with him was her worst decision. He really fucked her life up in ways you couldn't imagine. Raped because of him. Kidnapped and now this…" Lani told him, fighting back a sob. "Banko told her he was going to kill her. Bentley hustled for him and used to drive him around. Banko killed her, then he killed Bentley," she said matter-of-factly. Prince used his thumb to wipe her tears. "This is $25,000. I want you to have somebody kill him."

Prince looked up at her, his brow bent in confusion. "Have somebody kill him?"

Lani nodded. "I don't want it to be you," she whispered. "I don't want you to go back." They hadn't had any real time to connect, but even the thought brought an ache to her heart. Prince was her childhood crush, the first boy she had ever liked, lusted over, or loved, and she wanted a shot at his heart. Lani didn't like the feeling. It made her feel too delicate. She had messed with a handful, but she had never been in a relationship and didn't even know what he wanted or if he was into her or not. She couldn't afford to let her feelings mix with her grief because it would drown her. But right here on his lap, she felt like a woman. Like his woman. Like she could be herself – weak, emotional, and vulnerable – and he would make sure she was okay.

Prince's brow dipped deeper as she looked at him amorously. "I'ma be real wit you, Ma. I'ma kill him regardless." He spoke truthfully. "He owe me."

"He owe you?" Lani asked, frowning. "Money? I got money. I'ma make sure you getting…"

"Time, Ma." Prince cut her off. Obviously, Lani didn't know as much as she thought she did. "He owe me life. I gotta take his."

Lani shook her head slowly. "These niggas move to your beat. You're a Don. Why would you risk going back?" she whined. "I wanna get to know you. I wanna spend time with you. I just…"

Her throat was too constricted to speak. Lani could be the right woman for the right nigga. Prince knew anybody would jump at the opportunity to fuck with her, and he wouldn't mind the pleasure. But he couldn't let shit go. Until Banko was dead, he wouldn't be able to live, and having somebody else do it wouldn't quench his thirst for vengeance. It was personal, so it had to be done personally. Plus, he had killed Abby. That alone killed any chances they had.

"And after it's done then what? If you get caught, then what?!" Lani said, her voice raising an octave. "I used to see you around when we were younger, and you was God in my eyes. Looking at you now, I feel the same way, like you're you!" she told him, pouring out her heart. "You don't belong in a cage. You deserve to be out here running up a bag. Blowing that shit and getting your dick sucked on demand. Happy."

"This lifetime wasn't that for me, Ma," he responded. "I been killing people since I was thirteen years old. I been losing since then too. The people I love, my mind, my time." He paused. "The most dangerous shit I learned was how to control my emotions, so everybody think everything is good. Like the demons go away cause I made it home. Like I'm the happiest nigga in the world right now." Prince was letting it all out, and he trusted her with it. Venting to her felt safe and easy. "I'm ready to kill and die. I don't think that's the type of nigga you deserve."

"But why?" Lani cried, not understanding how someone with so much promise just wanted to throw it all away. "Why can't you make new plans? Why can't you make plans wit me?" she pleaded. "I never loved a nigga in my life because I was waiting on you! I didn't know I was, but I was because as soon as you sat in front of me, my fucking heart started beating for you!"

"Shit don't work like that wit me." He shrugged apologetically. "You wouldn't love me if you knew me," he told Lani as he leaned forward, his brown eyes looking into her gray ones. "I'm not the same nigga you had a crush on, Ma. The real me would make you hate me. If you was any bitch, I would of just played the game, fucked you, and kept it pushing. But for some reason, I won't let myself do you like that."

"Because you feel how I feel," Lani concluded. Her heart was beating so fast that she felt like she was going to have a heart attack. When she woke up that morning, she didn't think today would bring so much emotion. She didn't think she would lose her best friend and then be in her bedroom with the man she craved. "I want you. I deserve you. I don't care about anything. Nothing would make me change my mind," she said as she threw the money to the side and climbed off his lap. Lani kneeled in front of him, her hands on his lap as she looked up at him. "Fuck him! You say he owe you life, why give up yours? What did he do? Because I'm so lost right now, and I just wanna understand you. I just want a chance to be yours like I always wanted to be." She was putting her cards on the table – her heart in his hands – and she held her breath as she awaited his response.

Prince shook his head as he studied Lani. He removed her scrunchy, taking her hair out of its ponytail, and ran both of his hands through it as he pressed his forehead to hers. He had to keep her far because she was making him want to get close, and it was too early in the game for distractions. "He killed Dream," Prince disclosed, watching for her reaction. He had never told the truth, and by the look on Lani's face, she had never heard that. "He killed Dream, and I went down for it. They left me to rot in jail, and I did all that time. I only wanted to make it home, so I could kill everybody who left me for dead." Prince knew he was playing dangerous games. But he had to tell her, so she knew the real him. "I killed her."

Lani's world stopped. The sob that broke through her lips came from her soul, and her head found its home in Prince's lap. Lani cried harder than she ever did in her life as he held her head, rubbing her hair gently and looking out the window at the sky. Lani cried hysterically because her world was just turned upside down. Love and hate were the strongest emotions a human could have, and at that moment, they were both directed at the same two people. Her head spun, thinking about how Abby could stay with Banko after what he did. She thought about the times Abby had discouraged her from contacting Prince over the years. The lies. The fabricated story of a home invasion turned deadly and Prince being at the wrong place at the wrong time. Lani couldn't believe it. Then, Prince had killed her best friend. He just openly admitted it with no regret or remorse in his eyes or voice. Yet she still felt the same tenderness in her heart for him. The same yearning. She loved him. And at the same time, she fucking hated him because the truth hurt, and his truth just broke her heart. Lani's bawling was tugging at Prince's heartstrings. He didn't even know her, and something made him want to protect her and stop her tears from falling. He allowed her to let it out until she cried softly then looked down as she looked up.

"I hate you," Lani said, her voice cracking. "I hate Abby. I hate this whole situation." Prince continued to rub her hair, and the fact that he didn't snatch away at her harsh words made her want his touch more.

"For some reason, I don't wanna lie to you about anything or keep you in the dark," he told her. "I'm not gonna lie and tell you this whole Romeo, Prince Charming shit to explain it. I really don't know why, but there it is. The truth. The real me. I killed Abby and Bentley. If you still want me after that, then I know it's real."

After a pause, Lani stood to her feet, a scowl on her face as she stared into his eyes. Her mind told her to hate him, but her heart told her to love. The heart had a way of overpowering the mind every time, so she grabbed the bottom of her tank top then pulled the fabric over her head, revealing her perky breasts, then wiggled out of her sweats, exposing her nakedness, her bitch face still intact.

"I still want you. Nothing changed that," she said as she stood before him, naked, tears still spilling.

Prince admired her body. Her pussy was so fat it looked swollen, and the lips were glistening with juices. Her stomach was toned up due to her daily sit-ups, squats, and yoga, and her breasts were perky and perfect, round with pierced light brown nipples. He stood up and removed his clothes, standing in front of her in nothing but his socks. His chest made contact with her breasts, and his hands began to roam her body, sliding down her back then up her thighs until he was cupping her face. Her eyes captivated him, and the beauty mark on her cheek was in the perfect place. He wiped her tears. "You ain't gotta fear me or shit else in this world. If you could accept all that and still want me, be loyal, and suck my dick on demand," he said, causing her to giggle through her tears, "then I'm yours."

Lani didn't need time to think about it. "I'm not scared. I want you," she whispered as she stood on her tiptoes and pecked his lips

"I don't kiss," Prince told her.

Ignoring him, Lani took his bottom lip between hers and sucked on it before pulling on it with her teeth. Lani grabbed the back of his head and kissed him with fervor. Her womanhood clenched as he gripped her ass and sucked her entire tongue into his mouth. She broke the kiss, looking up at him, panting. He lifted her off the ground, and she wrapped her legs around his waist as he walked her to the bed, their lips never breaking contact.

Prince laid her on the bed, his body covering hers as they kissed hungrily, and his hands explored her body. Lani moaned when he squeezed her left breast, pulling on her piercing, and bit her bottom lip. The aggression caused a powerful tremor to run through her body, and her pussy became wetter as she arched her back, pressing her titties into his hand. Prince pulled back to look at Lani before burying his face in her neck, licking, kissing, and sucking as he traveled down to her collarbone, breasts, and stomach. Her hands touched everywhere he kissed then beat him to her throbbing love box. Lani palmed her pussy then let her open palm caress it, spreading her wetness along her lips and clit as she gasped then moaned.

The feeling of Prince watching her had her juices flowing like a waterfall, soaking her thighs, ass crack, and the sheet under her. Lani took the same hand she used to touch herself and ran it down Prince's mouth, coating his lips with her essence. Prince pulled back then licked his lips as he watched her play in her pussy and make the sexiest faces he had ever seen. Lani had never masturbated in her life, but she felt sexy doing it for him, and he had never eaten pussy before, but the taste of Lani had him addicted immediately. He kissed her thigh, sucking on it, leaving passion marks, until he reached her southern lips and kissed them tenderly, using his tongue to push into her. Lani's mouth fell open as Prince pulled back her labia, uncovering her clit. He swirled his tongue around her clitoris, flicking it before slurping it into his mouth and pulling back fast.

"Oh, my God, baby..." Lani cooed in pleasure, and her pussy excreted her natural juices, feeding into his hunger. He sucked her clit passionately, applying pressure, causing her body to climb near a climax. "It feel so fucking good. I wanna soak your beard…" she moaned out as she rubbed his head and watched him feast on her.

"You wanna soak my beard?" Prince looked up from between her thighs with a smirk on his face and her juices glistening on his mouth.

"Uh huh," Lani replied, amusement living in her eyes. "Your sexy ass," she said as her head fell back in pleasure as Prince pushed her legs behind her head, spit on her asshole, then licked until he reached her clit. He kissed up her body, palming her breast and licking her nipple before using his tongue to play with the piercing then biting on it.

"You ready for me?" he asked as he tortured her breast. She was in Heaven. This was already the best sex she'd ever had, and he hadn't even been inside of her yet.

"Yes… I want you so bad," she told him as she rubbed his face. She felt him press against her entrance, then they both gasped when he pushed in. Lani was so tight, wet, and warm that Prince had to brace himself as he lifted her leg and plunged into her depths. Her pussy was juicer than it'd ever been as he rooted himself as deep as her body allowed him.

Lani felt him touch the back of her pussy, filling her to capacity, and for the first time in her life, she orgasmed. Her pussy muscles clenched around him, gripping him tighter, as she dug her nails into his back and cried out. Prince stroked in and out, causing her to moan and groan. He picked up speed, every inch of his dick disappearing in and out of her wetness. Lani's pussy was A1 Steak Sauce – the best out there – and it was easily his favorite. He dug deep and grinded on her spot, kissing her lips and sucking on her tongue. He felt his nut building as Lani met him thrust for thrust. He folded her up, pushing her legs until her feet were by her ears.

"Oh, shit! Oh, my God…" Lani moaned. Her flexibility surprised and turned him on. He pounded her center for minutes until he was busting deep in her. Lani sucked on his neck, raked her nails down his back, and milked him with her insides. She never wanted this feeling to end, and from the feel of his erection, it wasn't going to anytime soon.

Prince pulled out, dragging every inch out slowly, as he pulled on her bottom lip with his teeth. Now he was on demon time. Every female wanted to be treated like a queen but fucked like a slut. Lani was no different. She laid there, smiling, as she watched him. His dick was covered in a concoction of their cum, and she wanted to taste it. She sat on her knees and lunged for him, pressing her body to his as she kissed him hungrily. Prince yanked her hair and spun her around. Lani arched her back as she lowered her chest to the sheets, busting her pussy wide open for a real nigga. Prince smacked her ass as she made it clap like a game of patty cake. Lani looked back at him, their eyes locking, both filled with lust and craving. She watched as he spread her cheeks then allowed his spit to drip from his mouth to her asshole. He landed a firm smack on her ass before leaning down and putting his face between her ass cheeks.

"Ssss..." Lani sucked in air as Prince pushed his tongue into her asshole. He ate her for a few minutes before kissing up her back and pushing himself inside her drenched box.

Prince gripped her waist with both hands and pulled her back into him. The sounds of her moans and pussy farting bounced off the wall as her ass bounced off his abs. He leaned over, gripping her chin, pulling her head back as he fucked her hard and deep. "Here, Ma." He directed her to open her mouth, and when she did, Prince allowed his spit to drop onto her tongue, and the act caused Lani to explode around his manhood.

Prince grinded into her, long stroking her for what seemed like hours, as Lani took it all, gripping the sheets above her head and cumming after every few strokes until he came inside her again. Prince pulled out slowly and turned her over onto her back before kissing her on her lips and lying next to her. Lani wrapped her arms around his neck as he pulled her as close as possible. "Today is the best and worst day of my life," she spoke into the crux of his neck. "I'm giving you my all. Whatever you did, you had to do. I'ma ride with you. Just never let me go."

A FEW HOURS AFTER A NAP, THEY PULLED UP TO THE BLOCK, AND IT was like nobody had left. Lani parked and cut the engine. "Loso is walking up on your side," she alerted Prince, her heart beginning to pound in her chest. This was the part that scared her, the part he told her to never fear. If it was up to her, they would still be in her bed. The conversation they had been having was essential. She wanted to know everything about him and wanted to help him through his loss. She needed him to know that she could be his rock and hold him down but more than anything, that she could lift him up. Prince looked at the rearview mirror. Loso was ten years old when everything went down, too young for them to run in the same circle. They had only met once, and Prince was sure people had filled his head with lies. But he didn't feel threatened. The same way that Lani had spotted him approaching, so did everybody else, and Gunboy, Kelz, Money, and Honcho were already in arm distance as the rest of the gang stood close by. Prince rolled the window down when Loso tapped on it.

"Whenever you ain't busy, I wanna chop it up." Loso leaned down and spoke through the window. He had always said he would kill him – that he would get revenge for Dream. But nothing made sense to him, and it wasn't until he got the call informing him that Abby was murdered that it became clear.

"Back up," Prince told him as he unlocked the door.

"Hey." Lani grabbed his hand pleadingly. Prince looked at her and squeezed her hand. She had vowed to ride with him, right or wrong, so she had to respect whatever happened. She sighed and let go of his hand then popped her lock and got out too. Prince stood on the side of the car, leaning on the door.

Loso looked over Prince's shoulder at Lani. Her riding with Prince also helped him come to his conclusion. "I always said I couldn't wait to we bumped heads." Loso sighed as he looked to the side at everybody who watched his every move. He had a few homies present, but he knew they had no wins if shit went left. "But now I see shit different." He stepped closer and leaned on the car, next to Prince, so only them two could hear what he had to say. "Banko sat in front of me and told my sister he was going to kill her. I ain't think nothing of it, and now she's dead." He sniffed back his emotions. "Either he did it or he had Bentley do it. Either way, I gotta kill him." Prince nodded as he stood quietly. "I don't think you killed my big sister. At first, everybody thought so. But a lot of people said you wouldn't have. Abby told me you didn't the day she found out you came home from jail," Loso revealed. "I didn't believe her. She said she couldn't tell me who did it but that it wasn't you. I want you to tell me who it was cause I don't have no family left, and I'm bout to be on demon time out here," he said as he wiped tears that were decorating his face.

Prince nodded at Kelz, letting him know everything was good, before he spoke to Loso. "Ain't my bop to speak no names. But I'ma handle that. You ain't gotta worry bout it," he replied. "I can't say I know how you feel. All I can say is that it's fucked up and handle your business how you see fit. If you feel like boy responsible, then ain't too much else to speak on. Let me know when and where he at." Loso nodded and held his hand up for dap. Prince could see the fire ablaze in Loso's light brown eyes and liked what he saw. That was the type of niggas he wanted around him – niggas who had nothing to lose and a lot to gain, who were capable of killing with no remorse. He dapped Loso.

"Son ain't even come to her memorial. After this, I'm on the hunt," Loso said.

"Don't tell nobody else that." Prince schooled him. "We gonna slide."

"I'M SO SORRY." CHERISH WIPED HER EYES AS SHE SAT ON THE COUCH with her best friend, Jordyn.

"Awwww." Jordyn hugged her, rubbing her back soothingly. "It's not your fault at all. It's mines for ever being over there." Jordyn shrugged. "Wrong place, wrong time, you could say."

Cherish shook her head and sniffed. "It's still fucked up. I'm glad you're okay. Did they catch the guy who did it?"

Jordyn shook her head this time. "No. I don't believe so." She paused. "I seen his face. Spoke to him before he did it. I'll never forget his face. He was cute. Young. He didn't mean to do it to me. So, I'm not mad at him."

"I was in there losing my mind, wondering why you wasn't answering my calls," Cherish spoke. "I knew it had to be something, and that drove me insane." They had been friends since Cherish moved to New York, and Jordyn had always had her back. In a way, she was glad that Jordyn wasn't purposely not answering her calls but was hurt that her friend had experienced trauma. "I met somebody while I was at court. He's the one that bailed me out."

Jordyn's eyebrow rose, confused. "Who is he?"

Cherish had been dating Jordyn's cousin for years, and the last thing Jordyn wanted was Cherish moving from bad to worst. "Have you spoken to Ghetto?"

"NO!" Cherish snapped. "Not one fucking time. Didn't even put money on my commissary. After everything I done for him."

Jordyn felt bad for Cherish. Her biggest regret was hooking them up. "You need to not forgive him. Now who's the new guy?"

"A real dude." Cherish nodded as she thought about Prince. "He just came home from doing a lot of time, and he told me he was going to bail me out. Then he did."

"You have to be careful, Cherish. Like who is he really? What was he locked up for? How was he able to bail you out?" Jordyn questioned, concern lacing every word.

"He's the one who helped me when I needed him. The one who kept his word," she replied defensively.

"Don't do that cause I would have if I could have!" Jordyn snapped back. She knew she wasn't supposed to be putting stress on herself, and the headache she felt reminded her that she had to take her pain pills.

"I'm not talking about you." Cherish calmed down, seeing the agony written on Jordyn's face. "I trust him. I slept with him last night and not once did he try to touch me. I feel it; he's different. We're just friends, and I got a good feeling about him," Cherish said sincerely.

"Well, I want to meet him," Jordyn said.

103

DIDDY INSPECTED HIS SURROUNDING BEFORE HE WALKED INSIDE THE building and up to the door on the left where Tammy was waiting on him. She had called him for some weed while the memorial was going on, and the look on his face made her want to console him. So, she had told him to fall through at three a.m. since that was the time Pun left for work.

"Shhh," she told him as she closed the door behind him then locked and put the chain on. She didn't know what she was doing with this young boy, but she was all for it. She directed him into the bedroom. Diddy walked into the pitch-black room and waited until his eyes adjusted before he sat at the end of the bed. He was nervous, and he hoped it didn't show. Tammy sat next to him and helped him pull off his shirt then kissed him on his lips. They kissed as he pushed her back and gripped her thigh. He sat up and removed his sneakers then his pants before dropping his drawers, leaving him butt naked. He kissed her some more as he pulled on her tights until they were on the floor. They scooted onto the bed, panting, as they made out, and just as Tammy grabbed his hard-on to guide him inside of her, somebody started banging on her front door like they were the police, causing them to jump up in shock.

"Tammy! Yo, Tam! Why the fuck is the chain on the door?!" That somebody was Pun. "Open the fucking door!"

"Oh, my God. Oh, my God," Tammy whispered as she quickly grabbed her leggings. Diddy didn't know what to do. Not having time to get dressed, he kicked them under the bed, but he couldn't fit under there himself. Thinking Pun came back because he forgot something, Tammy told Diddy to hide in the bathroom. Diddy closed the bathroom door as Tammy opened the front door. He could hear her arguing with Pun, trying to come up with a logical explanation. Something told Diddy to hide in the shower, and he was glad he did because the second he stood behind the opened shower glass, the bathroom door flung open, and Pun walked in before turning on the light and closing the door behind him.

CHAPTER 9

Three Days Later

"One time we was there, no lie, I seen him count like, fifty thousand in cash," Cherish whispered to Prince as she laid in the bed between him and Sin, who was snoring quietly at the other end. Jordyn had invited her to move in, but the last thing Cherish was trying to do was run into her ex-boyfriend. Plus, she felt safe in Prince's presence. Even Sin was cool, so she opted to remain where she was.

The palm of Prince's hands began to itch. He thought about the money Lani had offered him. The money Abby had offered as well. Although he needed it, he wanted to gain his own. He took from the gang because it was the least they could do. He had done the same for them indirectly and directly for years, but Lani and Abby's money felt like a handout. Him and Lani spoke about putting a play down and eating together. He was all for that because, from the look of it, shorty was eating five-star meals. The lick Cherish was putting him onto would be his first step.

"It only be him?" he asked, confused. There was no way a nigga touching so much money was so easy to touch. The lick seemed too good to be true.

Cherish nodded. "Uh huh and his aunt. It's like her apartment or something, and he only goes there to put money up. Him and my ex-boyfriend is close, so he trusted him."

"And so, he trusted you." Prince put the pieces together.

"I'm trustworthy," Cherish said defensively, her voice raising slightly. "If he wouldn't have left me the way he did, I wouldn't be doing what I'm doing. I would of took him breaking up wit me, but you don't just leave somebody who stood solid for you on stuck." She lowered her voice. Prince understood that more than anybody and had to respect how she was stepping.

"You right." He agreed with her. "How much you want out of it?"

"You gonna do me right," she responded confidently as she stretched like a cat in heat, almost kicking Sin. The jumpsuit she had on when Prince met her at court did well in hiding the dangerous curves on Cherish's body. Her stomach was flat, and her hips were wide. She had nice, perky, D-cup breasts, and although her ass wasn't fat, she had a nice, high, bubble butt that moved like it had a mind of its own. The way it bounced when she walked could make Stevie Wonder stop and stare.

Prince chuckled. "You got a lot of faith in a nigga, I see," he said, eyeing her as she turned over and laid on her stomach.

Cherish looked at him. "I do. You're the realest I've ever met," she said as she leaned over and pressed her lips to his cheek before turning over and putting her headphones in her ears. Cherish could feel his body heat, and it heated hers up. Her body was craving him, but she didn't want to jeopardize the genuine bond they were building. She had never been the aggressor or even this horny. She ran her hand from the back of her neck to her throat. She wanted to at least play with her pussy. A lump formed in her throat when she felt a hand land on her lower back. Goosebumps formed, and she prayed to God that he let his hands roam her body. She hoped Sin didn't wake up and interrupt either.

Prince watched as Cherish rubbed on her neck sensually and could tell she was dying to be touched. Her breathing was ragged, and she kept pressing her body into the bed, trying to get some form of friction. He thought about the fact that she had just came home and hadn't had sex in a while. He knew her pussy was tight and hot. Lani had fucked him good, but that didn't stop his dick from bricking up. He closed his eyes before he crossed the line, and their platonic relationship turned sexual. After a few minutes, Cherish felt a hand move inside her panties, rubbing her flesh. A low moan left her lips as the hand moved toward her pussy. Cherish was wet with anticipation as two fingers ran along her slit then pushed inside of her center. She was tight, and her juices drenched the fingers as her pussy engulfed them to the knuckle. She felt hot and soft as he kept his fingers pressed deep. Cherish bit down on the pillow as he slowly began finger fucking her. Her pussy made macaroni noises as he pulled out then in, bringing her pleasure. Her eyes shot open when she suddenly felt a hand grab her foot and discreetly place it on Sin's erection. There was no way that was Prince's hand. Sin pressed his hardness into her foot, and it caused her to explode all over the fingers inside of her, biting the pillow to keep from crying out. The fingers slowly removed from her, and Sin moved her foot, leaving Cherish at a loss for words.

Prince sat in the passenger seat of the Kia Optima Sin had borrowed from his shorty, .45 ACP gripped in his right hand and resting on his lap as Sin navigated through the streets. For the rest of the gang, this was just another come up, but for him, it was the start of his takeover. If this lick went right, it would put him exactly where he needed to be and show him what his niggas were capable of. Beastmode and Honcho occupied the backseat, all dressed in black with face masks and guns on them. Honcho had a gun connect, so he had an arsenal that they were able to choose from, and the guns they had chosen blew Prince's mind. Beastmode had a FN, and Honcho had a Glock .17 with an extended clip. The guns fascinated Prince, and he couldn't wait to get a chance to let them bark. They were on their way to the address in Bushwick that Cherish had told him about, and their trigger fingers and palms itched simultaneously the whole ride.

Out in the east, Kelz, Gunboy, and Nana were riding to another location with a different agenda, and if they were being honest, their hearts were heavy. This would be the hardest drill they'd ever gone on.

But a call was made, so it was either shoot or get shot. Nana hated what he had to do but understood his role, and he had no choice but to respect it after being informed of the reason behind it. As a real nigga, he knew he couldn't compromise his morals for anyone or anything. He was all in, so he was going to handle his business regardless of how he felt.

They reached their destinations at the same time and moved with no hesitation after surveying the block for potential witnesses. Prince casually walked toward the back of the building with the gang trailing behind him, and luck was on his side because a brick was placed to keep the door from locking. After they all walked in, he moved the brick then huddled in the hallway by the door the lick was supposed to be in. He looked at the time on his iPhone screen, 8:11 a.m. Cherish said the guy met her boyfriend here every Saturday at 8 a.m. and stayed until about 11 a.m. That was routine. Prince pressed his ear to the door and could hear a female voice not too far from the door. Then, he heard a male voice. His heartbeat increased. They had two options – wait until he came out or make their way inside. Prince lifted his fist and knocked on the door. They stood to the side as he heard the lady's voice approach the door. It was obvious that they were expecting someone, so Prince didn't waste any time. He lifted his arm and aimed the gun at her face as they pushed into the apartment. Sin and Honcho quickly moved toward the open area where a guy was sitting, counting money. The guy jumped up at the sound of footsteps and put his hands up in surrender as they walked his aunt into the living room at gunpoint. Tears spilled down her cheeks as Prince directed her to sit on the couch.

"Ya could have everything here. Nobody has to get hurt," the guy said.

Prince agreed. "That's a fact," he said as Sin began stuffing the money into the bag the guy had removed it from. "I want everything though. The money and the work." The guy knew the work he had there wouldn't hurt his pockets, and although the money would, he could make it back if he kept his life. There weren't too many people that knew he kept money here. Somebody definitely set him up.

"That's not a problem. I ain't tryna die over no money or drugs.

Everything in the safe under the kitchen sink. The code is 1-8-0-1." Honcho moved to the kitchen and located the safe before bringing it. "Shmoneyy, baby," he announced as he removed stacks of money, a Ziploc bag of white powdery substance, and another Ziploc bag of pills.

"That's everything?" Sin asked the dude.

"That's my word," the guy said.

"I want the watch too," Prince told the guy then watched as he took it off his wrist and handed it to Beastmode. "Now lay on your stomach, both of ya, until we…" A knock on the door interrupted him. Everybody stopped in their tracks. "Who you expecting?" Prince asked as he pressed the gun to the back of the lady, causing her to wince.

"A female friend. She just coming to pick up some money. She don't need to be involved in this," the guy stated, trying not to react to the sight of his aunt whimpering.

You want me to let her in?" Sin whispered. He was eager to show Prince that he was a demon.

The lick had gone easy thus far, and boy had been honest. So, Prince would take his word for it. "Na," he responded. "Grab his phone," he told Sin. Sin passed Prince the phone, and Prince had the guy unlock it then scroll down to the female's number. He had to put on his poker face when Nicole's number was pressed on, and he quickly added it up. This was Kelz's connect. Prince sent her a text as the guy, telling her he was rescheduling, then waited until he heard her leave before placing the phone in his pocket. He looked at Timbo and his aunt, and his trigger finger itched. Looking up, he locked eyes with Sin, who pressed his gun to the back of Timbo's head, waiting for the word to finish him off. Prince had given Kelz his word he would leave the plug alone, so he shook his head at Sin.

Nana stood with one foot on the wall, his gun gripped in his hand and by his side as Kelz sat on the steps leading upstairs as they waited. They knew he would be walking inside at any minute, and a part of them dreaded it. But he had made his bed. Now, he was going to lie stiff in it. They heard the screeching of the front door opening, and Nana took a deep breath as he stood straight. He gripped the gun tighter as he waited to see who they were waiting on. He always took the stairs, and today was no different.

"Oh, shit." He stopped mid-step when he spotted Nana. "What's poppin, buzo…" Nana raised the gun he had hidden by his thigh, aimed it at him, and pulled the trigger twice as his eyes watered up.

BOOM! BOOM!

Prince didn't know if he should let dude live. He had seen too many movies about motherfuckers finding out who you were then coming back to get you. His iPhone vibrated, snapping him out of his thoughts. He retrieved it and answered the FaceTime. It was Nana. "That shit done," Nana told him before hanging up the phone. Prince placed the phone back in his pocket and could tell the news hit everybody hard. He backed away from the lady and tucked his gun. They all turned and walked out without another word. They jogged to the car, got in, and Sin quickly pulled off, putting distance between them and the lick. The silence in the car was suffocating. They couldn't enjoy their gain because the loss hurt. Prince didn't regret making the call he'd made. It had to be done. But that didn't stop the tear that left his right eye. It hurt when you had to kill a nigga you loved. Or in this case, get him knocked off.

CHAPTER 10

Tiffany was laughing as she watched TV and stuffed her face with the scrambled eggs she had made for breakfast when she heard the sound of a gun going off. She jumped in her seat and almost dropped her plate. "What the hell?" she said as she placed her plate on the coffee table and grabbed her iPhone to look at the time. It was close to 8:30 a.m. "Money should of…" A lump formed in her throat, and her heart dropped to the pit of her stomach as she got up, wobbling as fast as she could toward the apartment door. She held the railing as she raced down the stairs to investigate, praying the whole way down it had nothing to do with her man. She could hear other tenants beginning to come out their apartments, but she had tunnel vision. She felt queasy, and it was like her baby sensed that something was wrong because he began to kick repeatedly. She reached the bottom of the stairs and froze in fear at her worst nightmare. She let out a blood curdling scream. There, in front of her, was Money, laid on the floor, a pool of crimson spreading beneath his body. "No!" she screamed as he gasped for air. He was choking as blood gushed out of his mouth and spilled from the bullet holes. Tiffany rushed over to him, dropping down to her knees and lifting his head onto her lap as he looked up into her eyes. "You cannot die. You hear me? You can't die." She sobbed. "Somebody call an ambulance please," Tiffany yelled out. Her mouth suddenly went dry, and everything began to spin. She could hear someone calling out to her, but she couldn't respond then. She fainted.

———————

CHERISH HELD UP A THICK WAD OF BILLS WITH A HUGE SMILE plastered on her face as Prince sat next to her, counting up the money, and she was amazed at all the stacks that sat neatly on the bed. He hadn't even counted it before telling her to take what she wanted, and she loved and respected him for that. She thumbed through the money in her hand, and it totaled $11,300. She was happy with that and knew it was enough to start her up. It was more than she'd ever had at one time. Prince rubber banded the last stack as he looked over the take with a smirk on his face, satisfied with the earning. They had come up with half a brick of coke, three hundred Percocets, and $56,000 after giving Cherish her cut. "If the world's wealth was distributed evenly, every living person would have this much." He nodded at the money. "Fifty-six bands."

"How the hell do you know things like that?" Cherish laughed joyously. Everything about him amazed her. He was handsome, smart, cocky, and bossed up. *And fucking sexy*, she said to herself as she thought back to the previous night. Cherish could still feel his hands on her, his fingers inside of her, and the feeling of Sin's hardness. She squeezed her thighs together to douse the fire threatening to burn her legs. Again, all she wore was a T-shirt and panties, and again, she felt the seat of her panties become wet and her nipples harden against her T-shirt. She noticed Prince noticing, and the sexual energy between them was thick.

"I like to know a little about a lot of things, so my conversation is versatile," Prince told her as he began dividing the money. "That's how you network." He put $16,000 to the side for himself, $10,000 for Nana, and gave the rest of the bros $6,000 apiece. He knew Sin had a flow with the dogfood and white girl, so he was leaving him and Beastmode in charge of the half of key and giving Gunboy and Honcho the pills. He quickly did the math in his head. Gunboy and Honcho would have to kick back two bands for the pills since they were going for $20 a pop, according to Cherish, and Sin and Beastmode would kick back $15,000 for the half brick. He was about to have his niggas on some real get money shit. "That shit ain't nothing though. We bout to really eat. This ain't the only jugg we gonna have. I got some shit cooking up, and I'ma put you on too, so you could always have your own bag as well. You a part of this shit just like everybody else."

Cherish looked at him, skepticism written all over her face. Her ex-boyfriend had told her the same shit a time ago. But that was never the case. Yeah, he had her getting a bag, but it wasn't for her independence. It was for his personal gain. Prince noticed the look on her face. "What's wrong?"

"Nothing." She pursed her lips, looking in his eyes.

"Use your words, Ma," he told her. She let out a breath of exasperation. The last thing she wanted to do was fuck up what they had. But if her ex did it, who was to say the next wouldn't?

"I don't mind doing whatever. Just don't shit on me. Please."

Now, Prince was confused. "Boy must have really fucked you up," he said bluntly, causing Cherish's shoulders to slump in embarrassment. "Ya relationship was ya business. I'm not gonna speak on it, but just know this ain't that."

"Anything I ever did was for his pockets. Anything I wanted, he never supported," she revealed as her eyes misted. "He wanted me to depend on him, so no matter what, I wouldn't be able to leave him. I want my own."

He couldn't understand how her nigga misused her. Prince shook his head. "Heard you. Shit different now. You do what you wanna do. Not what a nigga tell you to do cause you gonna be able to have your own money to do so," he said seriously. "You ain't gotta depend on nobody, but at the same time, I'm here if you need me. You band up right now. Go shopping, splurge, make yourself happy," he told her as his phone vibrated with a text from Lani. "I'm bout to have you jugging and finessing, touching bands on a regular," he told her as he texted back. "So, you could flex. Shit on whoever shitted on you," he told her. "And you don't owe me shit but loyalty."

Cherish nodded. Prince motivated her. When he walked in the door, she could tell something had happened that had dampened his mood,

but he put it all aside to just vibe with her. He never even brought up
the night before, and she didn't know if she should mention it or what
Sin had done. It wasn't like she was complaining. "You got my loyalty," she swore as she grabbed his hand. "I'ma ride or die wit you.
Anything you need me to do, I'm down."

"I need you to do what you want to do, and I want you to be smart
about whatever that is," he advised. "We gonna make this money, and
when it's all said and done, I just want you to help me invest it all.
Study shit that we could make millions off. Foreclosure housing,
stocks and bonds, shit like that. So, when I'm gone, you straight." He
squeezed her hand then stood up. He thought about Money's unborn
child. Even though Money had to pay for his sins, that didn't change
the love Prince held for him. Prince was going to make sure his child
would be financially stable. "It's a few people I wanna make sure is
good even when I'm dead."

"You're not dying no time soon. Please don't speak like that,"
Cherish pleaded.

"I'm ready to. Not on no suicidal shit but on some a nigga ready to
see what's next so I'ma live it up without worry. I'ma make sure you
super sturdy, and when I'm gone, there's a few people I want you to
make sure is sturdy. I'ma trust you that much."

———

DIDDY SHOOK HIS HEAD, BERATING HIMSELF FOR GETTING INVOLVED
with Tammy as he texted back-and-forth with her. His girl, Mercedes,
sat in front of him, telling him about her day, but he was too busy
thinking back to the day at Tammy's crib.

*Pun walked into the bathroom, flicked on the light, then closed the
door behind him before Tammy could get inside. She banged on the
door, telling him she had to pee, but he ignored her and dropped his
pants and sat on the toilet to shit, unaware that Diddy was standing
naked behind the shower glass. Luckily, when both glasses were
together, you couldn't see anything but a blur. Diddy held his breath as
Pun defecated and prayed he didn't get in the shower after he was
done. He could hear Tammy rushing Pun, yelling for him to let her*

Diddy knew he should have gotten dressed and curved the whole
situation, but he had been thinking with his small head instead of the
big one. Instead, he had fucked Tammy and spent the night. She had
put that grown pussy on him every night since, and he was hooked, so
hooked that he kept going back for more, taking the risk of Pun
catching him like Mr. Biggs caught R. Kelly.

"Did you hear what I said?" Mercedes asked, her lips pursed.
Diddy looked up from his phone and took her in. Mercedes was Sport's
younger sister. She had black hair, cinnamon skin, and a feisty ass attitude. They had been fucking with each other for years, and Diddy
loved her with everything in him, but he was young and still had a lot
to get out of his system.

"I heard you."

"So, what did I say?" she asked, looking at him with her eyebrows
creased. Diddy grinned and looked away. "See, you gonna make me
slap the dog shit out of you."

"Yeah, aight." Diddy grew serious. "Stop playing with me." He
looked around to see if anyone was watching them. Mercedes liked
putting on shows, and he definitely wasn't for it. They were sitting at
Buffalo Wild Wings, and the last thing he needed was unwanted
attention.

"Are you going to Abby's funeral with me?" she asked as she sat
back and rolled her eyes.

Diddy sucked his teeth. "I'm going to Kasper shit. That's big bro."
He bit his tongue to keep from saying what was really on his mind. In
his book, it was fuck Abby.

"We can go to both," Mercedes suggested. His phone alerted. and
he quickly typed back a message to Tammy. "Hello?" She reached over
and tried to snatch his phone, but he pulled back.

"Bro, fucking chill," Diddy spoke through clenched teeth.

"Why can't I see your phone? I'm not going to lie. Your brother came home and you acting real different, and I do not like it," Mercedes said, fuming. "That shit you did to my brother was out of pocket! Now you moving funny with your phone."

"Your brother crossed the line first," Diddy reminded.

"He ain't do shit the next nigga wouldn't have done. That had nothing to do with you. I been told you Sport is a snake, so whoever he bites, they deserve it," she argued.

"Nigga violate my brother, he violating me," he retorted. "Fuck your brother." Mercedes reached over and slapped Diddy. It took everything in him to keep himself restrained.

"Okay, here you go. Cheese fries with honey mustard wings..." The waitress came just in time. They glared at each other as she placed their food in front of them. Mercedes didn't even realize her acting like a little girl made him want that grown pussy more.

"You got saved by the bell. But I'ma have the last laugh."

PRINCE SAT ON THE RECLINER IN LANI'S BEDROOM, LOOKING OUT THE window with his thoughts all over the place. Lani had picked him up and brought him over to spend the night. They had watched a movie then talked until she fell asleep in his arms. He couldn't sleep though. There was a level of comfortability that he didn't know how to adjust to. The nightmares still came, and demons still haunted him, especially the new ones. Kasper and Abby's funerals were being held the next day and Bentley's the day after. But he wouldn't be attending any. To see Kasper in a coffin, stiff, would be his undoing. To see the others would be admiring his work.

"What's wrong?" Lani asked softly, concerned, as she removed the covers and walked over to him, naked. Her body was flawless, and she loved the look in his eyes when he admired it, so sleeping naked whenever he was present was mandatory. She stood between his legs, caressing his waves, as he kissed her navel.

"I'm good, beautiful." Lani swooned. She wasn't new to compliments and knew what she looked like, but his words of endearment were something different.

"No, you not. You sitting here thinking and tense. Let me ease it, baby," she told him as she pushed him back then leaned down and removed his boxer briefs before turning around.

Lani opened his legs, so she could fit between, and held onto his thighs as she slowly lowered onto his manhood. "Ahh…" she gasped as her face wrinkled in pleasure and pain. Prince bit onto his bottom lip as she took him to the hilt. She stayed rooted as he leaned up and kissed her shoulder. Lani leaned her head back as she grabbed the back of his neck and pressed her lips against his. Their tongues wrestled as Prince pressed her lips against his. Prince palmed her breast, pulling on her nipple. Lani broke the kiss and rose up until the tip was surrounded by her warmth then slid down slowly, creaming all over him.

Lani held her hair up as she moved her body like a snake, slowly rocking her hips and grinding as Prince licked up her spine and caressed her body. The full moon set the mood perfectly, and they both enjoyed the view as her pussy muscles contracted around his shaft. "This is your pussy, Daddy," she moaned out. Her head fell back in ecstasy as he sucked her neck and pinched her hard nipples.

"I'ma cum, baby." Lani could feel her clitoris swell as she came to an orgasm, drenching him in her cum. She bounced on him hard. Prince sucked in air as he gripped her hips at the feeling of her pussy placing him in a death grip. She looked back at him, biting into her bottom lip as she stared in his eyes and moved her hips in circular motions, ferociously grinding, then got up and straddled him, so they were face to face. She grabbed his neck again then let her spit fall into his mouth like he'd done to her the first time.

Prince swallowed then laughed, causing her to giggle and moan. "Nasty ass."

"That's cause of you." She gasped as she slid up and down slowly, gripping him and releasing him.

"Fuck," he groaned as his toes curled. Lani had that snap back because just like the first time, her shit was virgin tight.

"You ain't see shit yet." Lani gripped his shoulders as she bounced up and down, drowning him, until they reached a climax together. She leaned forward, resting her head on his shoulder as they caught their breath and stared out the window. "Let me hold you."

"Hold me?" Prince asked with amusement in his voice.

"Uh huh. You hold me; I wanna hold you too," she said as she slowly stood, wincing as they disconnected. She palmed her sore vagina. "Come shower with me, then you could lay on top of me and let me hold you," she told him as she pulled him to his feet. Prince kissed her and gripped the back of her neck. Lani was special. She was probably the only female who was able to force herself into his cold heart. "When the time is right, I'ma brag to the whole world that you mines," Lani told him as they stepped under the showerhead.

Sport didn't know what to do. He was getting money, plotting schemes, and popping bottles with new niggas that he didn't trust. He watched the dice hit off the side of the building and gritted his teeth when they landed. "Set it out, niggas," House announced to the other players. He picked up the few hundred and the dice then shook them. Sport had pulled up to hustle with counterfeit money, so it wasn't really a loss to him, but he had never had good sportsmanship, so it was pissing him the fuck off. "Next hit, I'm taking you shopping, sis." House gloated as he pointed at Keya. Keya laughed, but Sport didn't. His forehead dipped, and his entire body warmed. He grabbed the blunt that Booga offered him, took a pull, then passed it to Geek.

"Oh, word? You taking her shopping?" Sport asked as he nodded his head.

"With your money." House chuckled as he rolled the dice. House leaned down to read the dice, and Sport swiftly kicked him in the face. His kick resembled a field goal and dropped House, knocking a tooth out. Sport straddled him as he removed the gun from his waist then brought his gun up, only to smash it over House's face at full force repeatedly.

"Stop! Baby, stop!" Keya called out as a few dudes pulled him off. His shirt was covered in blood, and House's face was too. He laid on the floor in excruciating pain, spitting mouthfuls of blood onto the concrete.

"Empty that nigga pockets too," Sport told Geek as Keya held him back. "Move!" he barked at her as he pulled his arm free of her grasp. "I'm not playing with none of these niggas out here!" he barked out loud.

"Bro, chill." Booga approached him and stood in front of him. "We out before the cops slide through. You a wild nigga." Booga laughed. Sport grabbed the money from Geek and followed Booga to his car. His anger had gotten the best of him. He still hadn't bumped into Prince, and from what Nana had told him, Prince was on another level with shit. They had to talk asap because Sport was losing too much sleep overthinking. Tomorrow was Kasper's funeral. It wasn't the right time, but it was the right place. He could hear Kaya on the phone and then heard as she burst into tears. His first thought was that something had happened to his little sister, and he quickly turned in his seat.

"What happened?" Keya was hysterical as she passed him the phone. Sport looked at the phone before placing it to his ear. There was more crying. "Hello?"

Tiffany sniffed back snot as she tried to speak. "Bro, I'm in the hospital. Money got shot."

Nana drove nervously, constantly looking down at his phone and at his mother in the passenger seat. His palms were sweaty, and perspiration decorated his forehead. *Fuck did I do?* he said to himself. His mother had called him frantically, telling him to pick her up and drive her to the hospital. He had feigned shock when she informed him that Money had been shot, but the tears were authentic. He parked the car in front of Brookdale Hospital and got out then helped Gloria out. They rushed inside where family members waited in the waiting room. He hugged Money's mother, consoling her, and felt like a fraud. He didn't know what to do. His actions were both right and wrong in his opinion. Money had broken the code. He had become a snitch, but they were family. If somebody else would have pulled the trigger, blood would have been thicker than water. But in this case, water had to wash away the blood. He felt Money's mother tap him and looked up to see the doctor heading in their direction. He had shot Money twice in the chest at point blank range. There was no surviving that. So, he prepared himself for the screams and cries. But then, the doctor burst his bubble. "Your son is in critical condition and has fallen into a coma. But he is alive, Ms. Daniels, and we must be grateful for that."

CHAPTER 11

One Month Later
Prince cruised down the avenue in his black-on-black 2020 Bentley Continental GT V8 with the red interior, his right hand gripped the steering wheel as his left held his iPhone. The cocky smirk on his face couldn't be contained. In just thirty days, Prince had leveled up. The top gold grills in his mouth, the two Cuban chokers on his neck with the circular obituary medallion, and the 18K rose gold men's Nautilus Patek Phillipe on his wrist bragged for him. He was getting to a bag. Thirty days had felt like an eternity for Prince. Every day of his life was like a movie, and he was on his way to stardom. Instagram certainly agreed. He had only been active a week, and everything he posted had more hearts than Valentine's Day, and everybody was following. He wasn't with having his shit private because like Fab said, everybody who doubted was getting flexed on first, and everybody who hated was getting flexed on worst. He was the topic of conversation throughout the hood and borough, and Super Loyal had become the wave. They were getting money, all the bitches were on their line, and they were looking like rappers on social media. Everybody had leveled up, even Cherish.

While Lani was coaching the situation like Bill Belichick, Prince was quarterbacking it on his Tom Brady shit. He had secured the scamming lane, and anybody who was trying to jugg and finesse was trying to get next to him. At the same time, Nicole and Kelz had become the plug for the Zaza. Things were going good for the gang. Loso had come onboard, and although he wasn't a part of what they were building, he was contributing. Sport was doing him and officially linked with Booga Bread. Forever Famous and Team Self Made were calling themselves the Mets, which stood for My Entire Team Savages, and although there was tension, there was no static. They had their blocks they chilled on and their areas they frequented. The beef was on sight, but niggas were keeping the spinning to a minimum for the time being because any drill would definitely make the hood hotter than it already was.

With Money in a coma and speculation going around, everybody was on their toes, waiting for the summer to heat up. But for the most part, niggas were focused on a bag. Prince pulled up in front of the bank where he was meeting Lani and parked before killing the engine and pushing his door open. His blood-splattered Alexander McQueens touched the pavement as he stepped out of his whip dripped in Balmain jeans, a Christian Dior belt, and a white Dior T-shirt. His deep waves and thick beard were shaped to perfection, and his jewelry was blinding. Lani spotted him and took off in his direction, pouncing on him excitedly, giggling as he caught her in the air, groping her ass cheeks to hold her up.

"I missed you," she cooed as she pecked his lips and hugged him tight. He smirked as he placed her on her feet and wrapped an arm around her slim waist. Lani matched his fly effortlessly, and you would have thought they had picked their outfits out together. A green Goyard bag dangled from her arm, a white Alexander McQueen one-piece short jumpsuit hugged her dangerous curves, and she wore White Alexander McQueen sneakers on her small feet. Her long, silky hair fell down her back, stopping just above her ass, and a platinum Cuban choker adorned her neck. Lani looked damn good on his arm. It had been a few days since they had spent time together. Prince had been moving into his new three-bedroom apartment that he had leased and had been helping Cherish move into hers. Lani had helped him move in but then respected his need for space. She had been helping Cherish get situated instead and actually liked Cherish.

"I missed you," he said back as he kissed her forehead. "Everything good?" he asked as he looked up at the bank. This was the first time he'd ever gone inside of a bank to pull a jugg, but Lani wanted him hands on, front and center, establishing passive streams of income. The Maspeth Federal Savings Bank was located a few blocks from Lani's condo and was good enough to approve her grant and loan request without a second thought. They had approved $80,000, and Lani would see half of that.

"Of course." She pecked his lips again. "We got this." They both put on their face masks and walked inside. There weren't too many people inside the bank. Prince quickly counted six – three workers, two customers, and a security guard. They were called over to a teller, and Lani stepped into her role. Her mannerisms made it easy to see why she was so good at it. Working at a bank taught her everything she needed to know.

"Right this way." The Caucasian lady directed them. They were led into a small booth where they took a seat.

"After this, I gotta stop by my aunt's. I want you wit me," he told her as she squeezed his hand. This would be his first time seeing his Aunt Lisa. Lani was happy about that. Like Prince, she didn't rock with too many family members. Her sisters were the only ones she was close to actually. She knew seeing his aunt was important, and him inviting her meant a lot. She smiled brightly.

"This must mean you starting to love me." She stuck her tongue out at him.

"You don't think I love you?" he asked. He knew how he felt about Lani. He couldn't help it and wasn't trying to stop it. Although they had never spoken more about the title of their relationship or made it public, he was fucking with her the long way. With Lani, he was himself. They just vibed naturally, and it was what he needed. A lot of bitches had held him down, but Lani was the first to lift him up. She was also the first to actually hold him, and that was where he felt most confident. "I mean…" She shrugged shyly. Lani loved the time they spent together. She loved everything about what they had. Nothing mattered between them – not his clout, social media, or the money. It was genuine. He had become her best friend as well, and the last thing she was trying to do was apply pressure, but they agreed from the beginning that they would always speak what was on their mind. "You know how I feel about us, but you never tell me how you feel."

Before Prince could respond, the bank teller walked in with stacks of money. "Hey, I'm back." She smiled as she sat down. She pulled a money machine from under the desk and began placing each stack in it. Lani kept her eyes on the money, but Prince's attention was on the slightly ajar door to the manager's office. He could see the table covered in money. It had to be millions if he was guessing. Two armored truck workers walked out, and Prince got a better view. The sight made his dick hard instantly. He wanted what was on the table. That much money was only seen in movies. It made what the bank teller was counting seem frivolous. "Okay, it's a total of $80,000..." the bank teller told them as she placed purple bands around the stacks of ten thousand.

An hour later, after dropping Lani's car off at her crib, they were pulling up in front of his aunt's apartment in Brooklyn. Prince lowered the music. "Come on."

"I'm nervous," Lani admitted with a giggle. She had never had a serious relationship, so she had never met anybody's family.

Prince chuckled. "You take this dick, you could take a meeting with my aunt," he joked, causing her to laugh and blush.

"That's mine though. That's different," she said as she leaned over and gripped him through his jeans.

"Don't try to distract me, Ma. You coming inside," he told her as he got out. He walked around and helped her before leading the way to the apartment. He had texted his aunt on his way over, so the door was already open. They made their way inside and upstairs where he could hear voices coming from what he assumed was his aunt's bedroom. "Your favorite nephew is here!" he called out as he walked toward her room with Lani close behind him. He walked inside, and his heart stopped. A small baby took little steps until he was holding onto Prince's leg. Prince looked down at him then back up to a face he thought he would never see again.

"Hi, handsome." Angel wiped her eyes as she smiled at him. Prince couldn't even respond. He didn't know what to say.

This must be her son, he thought. Angel stepped forward, and Prince felt Lani step back. Angel picked up the little boy and stood in front of Prince.

"Say hi to Noah," Angel told him. "Noah, say hi to Daddy."

<hr>

"WHERE BRO AT? HE NOT ANSWERING NO TEXTS," GUNBOY SAID AS HE tried to call Prince. Covid-19 had shut down all the strip clubs, so they were supposed to link tonight and hit a hookah lounge, just the bros and a few of Lani's friends, then they would be sliding to the Poconos in the morning where they had rented an Airbnb for the next few days.

"He doing him," Caleb replied. Caleb had moved to Arizona a few years back, but he always kept it solid. Everybody loved Caleb. He was one of those dudes that just had good energy, so motherfuckers liked being around him. Bitches loved his lanky, six-foot four-inch frame and long hair. To see him back in the hood felt good.

Gunboy shook his head as he put his phone down then looked around the barbershop at Beastmode, Honcho, and Kelz. "Nigga fucking up the plan! I ain't ever been to the Poconos. If we ain't sliding, I'ma be aggy," he said as he picked his phone back up. He sent a text to Cherish to see where she was at. She was like a big sister to him, and they had grown close over the last month.

"Ayo, sup with Cherish? Nobody on that?" Caleb asked.

Gunboy's face soured in contempt. "Na, nigga, that's sis." He knew if Caleb wanted a bitch, he was getting her. But he was too loyal to go after anything the bros labeled off limits. "She's off limits." Everybody broke out laughing.

"This nigga on her body," Kelz cracked.

"On God, it ain't like that," Gunboy shot back. "That's really sis. She family, bro. Niggas fuck on her, then shit become weird. It's too many other bitches for that," he said seriously. His phone vibrated, and he looked down at the text. "She coming right now." Gunboy stood up and walked outside. He could see Cherish walking in his direction with another chick and turned to Honcho, who stood beside him. "Who you bringing tomorrow?"

"Might not go or I might see what's up with the light skin that C with." He nodded in their direction.

"Hey, bro," Cherish greeted Gunboy. "This my best friend, Jordyn." He turned, and him and Jordyn were both shocked when they locked eyes.

<hr>

Sport ordered his food then leaned against the counter as he scrolled through Instagram. "He came up. He came up good," he told Booga as he looked at a picture of Prince and Lani. Sport wasn't jacking the just friends thing. He knew Prince was fucking that. Booga scoffed as he passed his phone to his daughter. He had been on Lani for a long time. They had done business a time or two and had texted back-and-forth, flirting and talking, but it had never gotten any further. He couldn't lie; he was sour.

"I already been through shorty," he lied.

Sport looked up at him. "Word? Lani shit greases, huh?" he asked.

"Shit regular. She can't take it. Head game trash. Shorty just a big bag."

"A bag we need. Get next to her," Sport told him.

"You should of never fucked up that stitchy with House." Booga shook his head. "I'ma holla at my young boys."

"Fuck all that." Sport waved him off. "Holla at her. Abby dead, so you know Lani the one with all the sauce," Sport said as he spotted Nana walking into the Spanish restaurant. Booga spotted him too and tapped London as he moved his daughter behind him.

"Na." Sport shut shit down.

Nana chuckled as he walked in their direction and passed them to order his food. "Let me get white rice with beans, soft plantains. and pork chops," he ordered. "Wassup, nigga?" he spoke to Sport, who looked at him, grinning.

"I love you cause you a tough nigga." Sport laughed and dapped him. "What up wit Money?"

"Still in a coma." Nana kept it brief. Shooting Money had been weighing on him hard and was his biggest regret in life. He knew if Money made it, shit would get realer. "Sup wit you?" he asked Sport as he grilled London. He hadn't forgot that London was there when Chucky shot in front of his moms. *One day, I'ma get both ya pussy niggas...* he thought to himself.

"Regular shit, gang. See ya up. Put me on," Sport joked as he tapped Nana's chest with the back of his hand.

"Nigga, you the opp!" Nana joked back. "Na, but you know who you gotta holla at…"

"Fuck all that! You my nigga. You was my codefendant. Everybody else ain't shit to me. It's either niggas drill Diddy for what he did to me or…"

"You know that ain't happening," Nana cut him off.

"A long time ago, niggas all agreed if a nigga did wrong against the family or broke the rules, he was finished. Shit apply to everybody. Fuck make Diddy any different?"

That statement hit home for Nana. "You went against niggas, bro. You was fucking Mia knowing that bro was cuffing."

"Prince wasn't worried about that bitch. He ain't push no button over that. Diddy moved on his own. Only reason that nigga ain't dead yet is cause I been busy," Sport said harshly. "Open your eyes, bro. How he pushing a Bentley and most of y'all still walking? Nigga using ya."

"My nigga, cut it out," Nana told him. "That's bro, and that's that. We all family. All you gotta do is holler at him."

Sport stepped in close so only Nana could hear him. "You sure he ain't hit Money?" he whispered. "I'm smarter than a fifth grader, bro. He come home, Abby and Bentley died, then Money get shot? Come on, bro."

"I don't get what you tryna say," Nana said nervously as he grabbed his food and walked outside.

"Shit too close to home. Only thing that changed from the week before everything happened and the week it did was that he came home," Sport said as he followed him. "Either that nigga bad fucking luck or he got them hit. And if he did and you still riding wit him, I don't know who you are anymore, bro. Facts. Especially if he die. What about his son? Me and Keya had pulled up on Tiff a few days ago. Baby boy look just like Money."

The guilt was suffocating Nana. He grilled Booga, his daughter, and London as they walked out, and without thinking. he pulled his pistol off his waist.

"Fuck you doing?" Sport barked as he stood in front of Nana.

"Nigga, my daughter here!" Booga barked as he shielded her. His body filled with rage, and if looks could kill, Nana would have been on a shirt.

"How I know these niggas ain't hit him?" he asked through clenched teeth.

"Cause they don't know where he fucking live!" Sport told him as he pushed him back. "Put that shit away, nigga! You bugging the fuck out!" Nana bit into his bottom lip as he backed away and put the gun back on his waist.

"He backed me down in front of my daughter!" Booga spat, heated. Sport shook his head as he ran a hand down his face. Nana was his ace, and he wanted him on the same team. He knew Booga was going to want to get him back for that, and he couldn't really blame him.

"Ya shot at Sin in front of his moms." He tried to reason.

"Niggas ain't know that was his fucking mom!" Booga responded as they hurried to his car. "I'ma kill that nigga, bro! That's on everything. I'ma kill him."

Sport chuckled. "Nana a different type of demon. I don't think ya ready for his demon time."

Booga stared at Sport for a second before responding. "I don't think ya ready for mines.

EPILOGUE

Prince drove as music played throughout the car, and Lani sat silently in the passenger seat. What was supposed to be a quick stop was actually a hard blow. Seeing Angel was like an uppercut. But her dropping the bomb and claiming the baby was his was like a jab from Tyson. He knew Lani's mind was miles away, and her feelings were hurt, so he chose to let her be.

"You want me to take you back to Jersey or your sister crib? I'ma stop by Cleveland," he told her as he drove. Lani wasn't a block bitch. She had never been fascinated with just sitting on Cleveland Street or chilling amongst guys. The block was too mixxy for her liking, and the guys were too thirsty and had too much beef. But if that was where he was going, that was where she would be. Her feelings were hurt, but if what Angel was saying was true, not only did it happen before her, but there was nothing anyone could do to change it.

"Why can't I go wit you? I thought we was staying at your crib tonight?" Lani asked, feeling territorial. Her fears were being confronted, and she felt like them not making their relationship public gave a bigger opportunity.

"I'm not sure what you wanna do cause I'm sure you in your feel-ings," Prince responded, understanding the weight he'd just placed on her heart.

"I am. But not in a bad way." She paused. "If he's yours, then we gonna make sure he's straight. He's our responsibility too."

At that moment, Prince realized he really had the realest bitch on his arm. "I love you. Real shit. I love you."

Lani beamed, and her heart skipped a beat. To hear him say those words for the first time was bliss. "I love you," she said emotionally. "Do you think he's yours?"

"I made shorty into a woman. I instilled certain morals in her that I could never question," Prince admitted. "I can't even lie. I felt a connection when he grabbed my leg." Lani nodded. She was happy for him but sad that someone else would have a lifetime tie to him. Prince could feel her sadness oozing out of her pores and into the air between them. "This shit blindsided me, but I can't lie like I ain't happy about it. Shocked but happy cause me and her dreamed that together," he said verily. "I ain't never thought we wouldn't be together cause it's always been us. We had years together. But it ended, and I don't regret the ending cause now it's me and you. I know this ain't what you wanna hear. but I'ma always love her. If she gave me that, then I'ma always love her too. But with you, that's where I wanna be. I'm tryna build a home. Just give me time. I'ma make you the happiest woman in the world."

"I don't want this whole perfect love story. I just want a real one," Lani said. "I'm happy wit you. So, none of it pushes me away. We can't do anything but what's supposed to be done, and I respect you being a real one. If you didn't wanna hold her down, then I'd look at you different, you know? We got this. I told you; I'm riding and dying with you," she told him as she interlocked her fingers with his and looked down at her bag. "We got a forty pack right here right now. We can give her five for him. Now that it's a little realer, we gotta be smart. I ain't seeing what I normally would see monthly off the laundromat, and I only got about $35,000 put up. You know my checks from my job pays all the bills." Prince admired that. There weren't too many people he knew who had that much, and Lani made it seem like it was peanuts. He knew she owned her own laundromat, her car was paid off, and she was damn near done paying off the condo. She was already set, and he felt like he was adding baggage to her life.

"You ain't gotta do that, Ma. I'ma do my part. I got like $15,000 put away." Right then, he began to think of sources of income.

"We a team, so it's not me and you. It's us. Which means we gonna do our part. Any part you need me to play, I'ma play," Lani said seriously.

"You got game," Prince said as he looked over at her, causing her to laugh. What she didn't know was that Angel wasn't jacking any of that. "I'm serious though." She blushed. "And I'm serious about you, which is why I took you wit me," he told her. "Don't think that I'm not cause we ain't out there. I ain't hiding you, Ma. I'm just tryna get so much in order, then it's all about us. I'll let the world know."

Lani smiled as she leaned back and looked out the window. Prince had her heart, mind, and soul, even after his last breath. All Lani wanted and needed was him, and she was willing to prove that as long as he remained real.

They rode in silence until they reached Cleveland Street. Prince's phone rang as he parked, and it was just the call he was waiting on. He answered and accepted the call. "What's the vibes, gang?"

"You the vibes, my guy. Talk to me." F.L.'s voice came through the car speaker. Prince had emailed him, telling him to call asap. He knew F.L. could get a bunch of inmates to give up their personal information, and Prince would be able to finesse it and file an unemployment claim, making them a few bands each. Before he could get into details with F.L., he noticed a lot was going on in front of the barbershop. Prince's brow creased.

"Hold up, gang," he told F.L. then turned to Lani. "Stay here," he told her as he opened the door and got out.

"Bro, let her the fuck go!" Cherish yelled at Gunboy as he bear hugged Jordyn. She turned to Prince and looked at him with pleading eyes. "Stop him."

"Yo, wassup, gang?" Prince asked. He wouldn't stop him because it wasn't his business.

"I just wanna talk to her, big bro," Gunboy pleaded as Jordyn struggled to get out of his grip.

"Talk? Boy, please! Let me go so I could leave," Jordyn yelled. After recognizing Gunboy, she had hauled off and slapped him, the flashback of the shooting playing before her eyes in slow motion. She turned to leave, but he wouldn't let her go. Gunboy remembered locking eyes with her before he squeezed the trigger and could now see the scar on her face that his bullet had left as a reminder. He instantly felt bad, and the feeling was foreign. Usually, whoever caught the bullet could eat it.

"I'll let you go if you talk to me," he told Jordyn as he pulled her toward the building. She started to curse him out and pull his hair, causing a huge commotion. "Get him off my friend!" Cherish demanded.

Truthfully, she was beyond confused. She didn't know how their worlds had crossed. but along the lines, it did, and it wasn't in a good way. She didn't know what to say or do.

"He's not gonna hurt her," Prince told Cherish, halting everyone from intervening. He didn't know what beef they had, but he wasn't playing Captain Save a Hoe, especially when with as much fight as Jordyn was putting on, she wasn't really trying to break free.

"I just wanna talk." Gunboy struggled to hold her. As petite as she was, Jordyn was stronger than expected.

"Talk for what?" she asked. "You fuckin shot me in my face!" she hissed loudly as she stopped struggling. The words caused him to release pressure, and it seemed like time stood still. They stared in each other's eyes, and his hand went to her face, tracing her scar with his thumb. Jordyn sucked in her air and held her breath. He was the last person she thought she would ever see. He deserved the slap, but she wouldn't broadcast why she slapped him because she knew the bullet was never meant for her. As he rubbed the scar, her tears threatened to spill. There she was, face to face with the man who had almost killed her, but it seemed like the shock and paranoia she suffered since the day she was released from the hospital strangely evaporated when he grabbed her. She couldn't feel safe in the arms of her shooter. This had to be a type of Stockholm Syndrome. Jordyn's anger intensified, and she pushed him off then brought her arm up before bringing it down and smashing him on his head with the Snapple bottle she had in her hand, shattering the bottle. Gunboy's eyes went wide as he stumbled back, and the gash began to pour blood into his braids.

"Leave the block before I do something else I'ma regret," he told her through clenched teeth. Jordyn stared at him for a full second before turning and storming off, but before she could pass him, Prince grabbed her wrist tightly, causing her to stop and look up at him.

Cherish hesitantly took a step forward. "Prince…"

"Na, big bro," Gunboy called out as he used his shirt to stop the blood from spilling. Prince let her go and watched as Cherish followed her, trying to get information.

"What happened?" Prince questioned Gunboy. Gunboy touched the gash on his head as he watched her walk away.

"I did bad."

Prince shook his head. "You niggas gotta get it togetha." He turned his attention to Jordyn's car as they drove off. He didn't know what was going on and didn't care as long as it didn't pose a threat or distract Gunboy from what they had going on. Prince needed his niggas focused because he wasn't planning to lose.

To Be Continued…

Bandemic 2
Coming Soon

Did you enjoy the read?
Let us know how much by leaving us a
review on Amazon and Goodreads.

OTHER BOOKS BY

Urban Aint Dead

Tales 4rm Da Dale

The Hottest Summer Ever

Hittin' Licks For The Holidays: Atlanta

Wet Dreams On Lockdown: The Nurse

How To Publish A Book From Prison

How To Invest In The Stock Market From Prison

By **Elijah R. Freeman**

Despite The Odds

Despite The Odds 2

By **Juhnell Morgan**

Good Girls Gone Rogue

Good Girls Gone Rogue 2

By **Manny Black**

Hittaz

Hittaz 2

Hittaz 3

Hittaz 4

Hittaz 5

Hittaz 6

Coldhearted

Coldhearted 2

Coldhearted 3

By **Lou Garden Price, Sr.**

Charge It To The Game

Charge It To The Game 2

Charge It To The Game 3

A Summer To Remember With My Hitta

Snatched Up By A Hitta

Santa Sent Me A Real One For Christmas

Wet Dreams On Lockdown: The Unit Manager

Thug Me The Right Way 2

Thug Me The Right Way 3

Seizing A Gangsta's Heart For The Summer

Yours For The Taking

Wrapped Up In A Hitta's Love For Christmas

By **Nai**

A Set Up For Revenge

A Set Up For Revenge 2

Wet Dreams On Lockdown: The Librarian

By **Ashley Williams**

Trickin' On A Heaux For Christmas

Homie Hoppin' For The Holidays

Wet Dreams On Lockdown: The Female C.O

Letters Of His Love

By **Telia Teanna**

The State's Witness

The State's Witness 2

The State's Witness 3

This Time Won't You Save Me

This Time Won't You Save Me 2

His Summer Side Piece

IN The Streetz

IN The Streetz 2

IN The Streetz 3

IN The Streetz 4

IN The Streetz 5

By **Tron Hill**

Hittin' Licks For The Holidays: New York

By **Freshh Moneyy**

Coming Soon From
URBAN AINT DEAD

Drill
The Hottest Summer Ever 2
THE G-CODE
Tales 4rm Da Dale 2
How To Build Your Credit From Prison
By **Elijah R. Freeman**

Good Girls Gone Rogue 3
By **Manny Black**

Despite The Odds 3
By **Juhnell Morgan**

Wizdom: Forever Your Gangsta
By **Nai**

The Promissory
This Time Won't You Save Me 3
By **Kyiris Ashley**

Atlantastan 3
By **Chris Green**

IN The Streetz 6
By **Tron Hill**

Bandemic 2
By Freshh Moneyy

ASSISTED PUBLISHING PACKAGES

Bronze Package

- Includes:
  - Cover Design
  - Editing
  - Formatting/Typesetting
  - Publishing Consultation
  - Price: $400

Silver Package

- Includes:
  - Cover Design
  - Typing
  - Editing
  - One Flyer
  - Formatting/Typesetting
  - Publishing Consultation
  - Price: $725

Gold Package

- Includes:
- Cover Design
- Typing
- Editing
- Proofreading
- Two Flyers
- Formatting/Typesetting
- Copyright Registration
- Publishing Consultation
- Amazon Upload
  - Price: $975

Platinum Package

- Includes:
- All-in-One Bundle: Typing, Editing, Proofreading, Formatting/Typesetting
- Cover Design
- Three Flyers
- Publishing Consultation
- Copyright Registration
- Amazon Setup & Upload
- One Month Promotion
- Amazon Setup/ Upload
  - Price: $1,200

Individual Services

1.Editing Services
   - Proofreading: $100
   - Manuscript Editing:
   - 0-60k words: $350
   - Contact for a quote for manuscripts over 60k words.

2.Manuscript Preparation

•Formatting/Typesetting: We will prepare and arrange your book's text and interior for printing.
    •Price: $100

3.Design Services
    •Cover Design: $100 (2 free revisions, any additional revisions will be an additional cost)
    •Promo Flyer: $25
    •Custom Flyer: Contact for quote

4.Distribution Services
    •Amazon KDP Setup: $25
    •Amazon Upload: $25 (if you already have an account but just need us to upload it for you)

5.Other Services
    •Typing: $300 for manuscripts up to 40k words (Contact for quote for longer projects).

    •Copyright Registration: $100 + site registration fees.

U.A.D PROMOTION PACKAGES

<u>Tier 1: The Basics Package</u>

Price: $99

Target Audience: First-time or budget-conscious authors seeking minimal exposure.

Perks:

- Social Media Shoutout: 3 IG Story posts a week for a month.
    - Inclusion in Newsletter: Mention in the "Sponsored Showcase" section with a link to the book.
    - Digital Promo Graphic: A simple branded image featuring the book cover for the author's use (i.e. Available Now flyer)
    - Support Sunday Link In U.A.D FB Group: Book cover and link in Support Sunday post in group (x4)

<u>Tier 2: The Spotlight Package</u>

Price: $199

Target Audience: Authors seeking increased visibility for their release.

Perks:

- Social Media Shoutout: 3 IG Story posts a week for a month.
  - Inclusion in Newsletter: Mention in the "Sponsored Showcase" section with a link to the book.
  - Digital Promo Graphic: A simple branded image featuring the book cover for the author's use (i.e. Available Now flyer)
  - Support Sunday Link In U.A.D FB Group: Book cover and link in Support Sunday post in group (x4)
  - FB Group Promo: Book posted Monday-Friday in over 20 Urban Reader FB Groups for a month.

Tier 3: Maximum Visibility Package

Price: $299

Target Audience: Authors seeking an increased promotional push.

Perks:

- Social Media Shoutout: 3 IG Story posts a week for a month.
  - Inclusion in Newsletter: Mention in the "Sponsored Showcase" section with a link to the book.
  - Digital Promo Graphic: A simple branded image featuring the book cover for the author's use (i.e. Available Now flyer)
  - Custom Quote Graphic: 3 Eye Catching Quote Graphics that can be used on Social Media.

- 3 To 5 Character Visuals: Visuals of the characters in your book that can be used for promo.
- Support Sunday Link In U.A.D FB Group: Book cover and link in Support Sunday post in group (x4)
- FB Group Promo: Book posted Monday-Friday in over 20 Urban Reader FB Groups for a month.
- Paid Ad: We will run an Ad for your book for a month on a Sponsored Showcase page with a customized caption, targeting your book's audience to grow your readership.

BOOKS BY

URBAN AINT DEAD's C.E.O

<u>Elijah R. Freeman</u>

Triggadale 1, 2 & 3

Tales 4rm Da Dale

The Hottest Summer Ever

Murda Was The Case 1, 2 & 3

Hittin' Licks For The Holidays: Atlanta

Wet Dreams On Lockdown: The Nurse

How To Publish A Book From Prison

How To Invest In The Stock Market From Prison

STAY CONNECTED

Follow
Elijah R. Freeman
On Social Media

FB: Elijah R. Freeman
IG: @the_future_of_urban_fiction